What Happens in Vegas...

Second Edition

What Happens in Vegas...

Second Edition

Mike Faricy

Library of Congress Control Number: 2023914847
paperback ISBN: 978-1-962080-19-4
e-book ISBN: 978-1-962080-20-0

MJF Publishing books may be purchased for education, Business, or promotional use. For information on bulk purchases, please contact the author directly at mikefaricyauthor@gmail.com

Published by

MJF Publishing
https://www.mikefaricybooks.com

To Teresa
"You're a right plonker!"

Acknowledgments

I would like to thank the following people for their help and support:

Special thanks to my editors, Kitty, Donna and Rhonda for their hard work, cheerful patience and positive feedback.

I would like to thank Ann and Julie for their creative talent and not slitting their wrists or jumping off the high bridge when dealing with my Neanderthal computer capabilities.

Special thanks to Ann for her patience.

Last, I would like to thank family and friends for their encouragement and unqualified support. Special thanks to Maggie, Jed, Schatz, Pat, Av, Emily and Pat for not rolling their eyes, at least when I was there, and most of all, to my wife Teresa whose belief, support and inspiration has from day one, never waned.

One

Goose was an old hockey buddy of mine, and we'd been deployed together. He'd pulled me out of a firefight along with four other guys in our squad. Fought his way in to help us, and then we fought our way back out. He got a Bronze Star for valor for his effort, although if you ever brought it up, he'd just smile and change the subject. I hadn't seen him for close to five years. He'd bounced around ever since we made it back stateside. Last I heard, he was working construction, but that was obviously out of date.

"I, I gotta be honest, Dev. You're really kind to offer, but it's not like I can pay you. I went out to Vegas about eighteen months ago. My mom was worried about my younger brother, Kenny."

"Kenny's out in Vegas?"

"Yeah, you remember he's got Aspergers. Always had this thing for statistics and numbers, that sort of stuff." He drained his beer, and I signaled Jimmy for another round. We'd been sitting in The Spot for a couple of hours, just catching up with the usual 'Who's doing what to whom' sort of talk. Morton was napping at my feet after devouring a bag of pork rinds.

"He went out to Vegas to seek his fortune. My mom was worried he'd end up with the wrong crowd or, worse, dead. So I went out there with the idea of talking him into coming back home. The next thing I know, I've been out there for a year and a half."

"Is he okay, Kenny? What's he doing out there?"

"He works for one of the casinos, a place called The Palms."

"The Palms? I don't think I've ever heard of it."

"It's a good mile from the strip. I suppose the Bellagio or Caesars would be the closest places, but they're probably a fifteen-minute cab ride away. The Palms has a reputation for being a party place."

"A reputation for being a party place? In Vegas? What the hell does that mean?"

"It can get crazy. Fortunately, Kenny's not involved with any of that. He's in a quiet room all by himself working on numbers and percentages, and loving it."

"So what are you worried about?"

"There are these three guys, a combination of want-to-be made guys and dipshits. They've been trying to buddy up to Kenny, and I can't see anything good coming from it. I was hoping you might have some P.I. connection out in Vegas, maybe put in a good word for me, and I could get them to check these scumbags out."

"I honestly don't know anyone out there, Goose. But I tell you what. I've been getting pressure from a *friend* to take her someplace fun. She didn't really get off on my idea of a weekend in Minneapolis. Maybe a few nights in Vegas would do the trick."

"Man, Dev, that's really nice of you, but like I said, I can't pay you. Tell you the truth, I just don't have the cash."

"I don't recall saying anything about being paid, Goose. Maybe call it payback."

Goose looked the other way, took a quick sip from the fresh pint Jimmy just slid in front of him and changed the subject. "It gets hotter than hell out there in the summer."

"We've been in hot places before, Goose, and we're here to tell about it, thanks to you. I'll get out there, and I don't want to hear another word about it. I owe you, man."

"Dev, I didn't mean you had…"

"Goose, I owe you, enough said. Now, have you been following the lousy year the Twins are having?"

We sat there for another hour, then climbed into my car. Goose was catching a redeye back to Vegas, and I was giving him a lift to the airport.

"You've gotta be kidding me, man. You think this thing's going to make it out to the airport and back?" Goose asked. It was his first introduction to my car. He had just opened the rear door for Morton to climb into the back seat, then tossed his suitcase in.

I couldn't really disagree with him. I was driving a 2010 Ford Escape. The thing had four cylinders, no pickup, the air conditioning didn't work, and the engine had a tendency to just shut down if I pushed it over sixty. If anything, I needed an escape from my Escape.

"Hey, I suppose you could grab a taxi for thirty-five bucks if that would make you feel better. You could walk, but then you'd probably miss your flight. Or you could just shut the hell up," I said, then turned the key in the ignition, and we listened to the engine groan.

"What's that smell?"

"It's just a little exhaust, let's me know the engine's running. Soon as we get moving, I'll put down the windows, and it'll air the place out."

"God."

"I just gotta let the engine warm-up for a minute or two, and we'll get going."

Goose shook his head, then said, "Mind if I ask you something?"

"It was what I could afford at the time, okay? I got a deal, kind of."

"No, I wasn't thinking about this bomb. Matter of fact, I don't want to know any more about your car. You told me once you had a relationship with a mob guy or someone here in town. I can't think of his name, something like Jumbo or Biggie."

"Oh, you mean Tubby Gustafson. Yeah, I sort of know him and try to stay away. We've maybe helped each other out over the past couple of years. I know his main guy, Fat Freddie Zimmerman, too. Pulled his feet away from the fire more than once."

"Perfect. You think they might have some connection out in Vegas? Someone who could maybe help me out?"

"Help you out? You mean with these guys hanging around Kenny? I don't know, I think Tubby pretty much deals with just St. Paul stuff." The last thing I wanted to do was have any interaction with Tubby Gustafson, or, for that matter, Fat Freddy. It never seemed to work in my favor.

"Oh, okay, I was only wondering. There's an ex-cop I work with, heads up security at the Bellagio. I'll see him tomorrow. Maybe I'll just check with him and see if he has any ideas."

"That makes more sense. I think Tubby stays pretty close to home. He's got enough on his plate without going all the way out to Vegas." Bullet dodged, I figured, and pulled away from the curb.

"Hey," Goose coughed. "You think you could find it in your heart to lower the windows I'd like to not be asphyxiated when we pull into the airport."

"Oh, yeah, sorry about that," I said and pushed the buttons to lower the windows.

"What the hell is that red light that just came on the dash?" Goose asked a minute or to later.

"Relax, it's just the check engine light. The thing always comes on after a few minutes."

"You ever think about getting this thing checked out?" Goose sounded worried.

"No, the check engine light just refers to the door locks or the windows or something. Relax, we're almost there," I said. I put my blinker on and began merging onto the exit for the airport. Suddenly, the engine started making a rumbling noise. "Oh, that's not good."

"Oh, Jesus," Goose whined and looked worried.

The engine made a louder sort of rumbling noise, then shut down altogether. I coasted over onto the shoulder of the road, then rolled along for maybe a hundred more yards before we came to a stop.

"Sorry, man, I think you'll have to hoof it from here." We were no more than a block away from the main terminal.

Goose just shook his head, then grabbed his suitcase out of the back seat. "Let me know when you're coming out to Vegas, and Dev…"

"Yeah?"

"Ditch this beast. Good seeing you, man," he said, then started walking along the shoulder of the road toward the main terminal.

I watched Goose slowly walk out of sight, then waited another ten minutes, fired up the Escape, and prayed we'd make it home.

Two

I was sitting at my desk the following afternoon, looking out the window with my binoculars at the apartment across the street. The girls in the third-floor unit were scurrying around in thongs and hair curlers, getting ready for some event. Both of them were sipping from wine glasses, occasionally eating a cracker with cheese, and in general, just taking their time, which was fine with me, I was enjoying the view.

Apparently, I was a little too focused on the activity across the street. I heard someone clear their throat, and when I turned around Fat Freddy Zimmerman and Tubby Gustafson were already seated in the client chairs on the opposite side of my desk.

"Solving another crime, Haskell, or thinking of committing one?" Tubby said. He tossed a square of chocolate in his mouth and threw the wrapper on my desk.

"Oh, Tub— I mean, Mr. Gustafson, what a nice surprise. How can I help you, gentlemen?"

Fat Freddy looked at Tubby for a long moment until Tubby gave him a nod. "We received an inquiry earlier this afternoon," Freddy said.

"An inquiry? Something I might be able to help you with?"

"We understand you have contacts in Las Vegas, and they've been— inquiring about us?"

"Las Vegas, I haven't been asking anything— Well, I do have a friend out there, an old high school pal and army buddy. He was back here for a couple of days, visiting his mother. We got together, one thing led to another, he asked me to help his brother in a very minor matter, and I haven't been to Vegas in a number of years so I thought I'd go out there, just for a night or two, you know, and—"

"Haskell, you twit, shut the hell up," Tubby yelled. "I don't have the patience for any of your stupid games today, or any other day, for that matter. Now, why in the hell are you having someone ask questions about me out in Las Vegas?"

"Yeah, Haskell. What the hell is that about?" Fat Freddy said and followed up with a sneer.

"I, I didn't tell him to ask any questions about you. Honest, I didn't. He must have somehow put it together that we knew one another, that I had done some work for you and—"

"Done some work for me? You can't be serious. Done some work for me? Did you hear that, Freddy? The last dealing we had was in reference to you lending your car and a gun to that fool who held up my card game. If I recall, my contract with you was something along the lines of letting you live, provided you delivered that idiot to me in twenty-four hours."

"It was forty-eight hours, sir, and—"

"Haskell! There you go again. I guess that's what I get for being generous. More of you putting your nose where it doesn't belong. You think I want people to know I've associated with the likes of you?"

"Well, sir, it's just that—"

"Silencio! You half-wit. All right, here is what you're going to do. In short order, I want your sorry ass out in Las Vegas. You're going to deliver a message, in person, to this idiot friend of yours, telling him to stop asking questions about me. Then you're going to get that numbers-obsessed loon at The Palms, Kenny Gander, to accept my offer." Tubby suddenly groaned to his feet. "And because I'm overly gracious and never seem to learn from my mistakes, you've got until the end of the week, Haskell. The end of the week, or so help me, you'll be hearing from me, and next time I won't be this pleasant."

"What offer? I don't know anything about an offer to Kenny."

"Haskell, so help me. You try and play me for a fool, and I'll have your head. Instead of window-peeking on two naked women drinking wine and eating a cheese ball, I'll have you thrown out of that window." He reached into his suit coat, pulled another foil-wrapped chocolate out, tossed the wrapper at me, the chocolate into his mouth, and stormed out the door.

Fat Freddy stood, gave a shrug, shook his head, and headed out the door.

It dawned on me that I never mentioned Kenny's name. That meant that Tubby was a lot better connected out in Vegas than I ever thought. Goose would have landed around four this morning, probably had a noon shift. And, with the time change, less than three hours later, Tubby's in my office threatening to have me thrown out the window. And by the way, how in the hell did he know I was watching two women, and that they were eating a cheese ball?

I picked up the binoculars and scanned the third-floor apartment across the street. The girls were nowhere to be seen. What remained of the cheese ball sat on the kitchen counter, next to two empty wine glasses. I waited for the next twenty minutes, hoping maybe they were going to return, but neither one of them ever reappeared. Tubby couldn't have an in with them, could he?

I'd have to figure something out fast. That something was going to have to be a trip out to Las Vegas. Not my most favorite place in the world, but then again, Tubby had presented a fairly persuasive argument.

Three

Where to begin . . . Her name was Barbara Millicent Dahl. I called her Barbie. She referred to herself as Barbie Doll. Yeah, the chick with the pink house, the pink car, best friend named Midge, sister named Skipper, and a boyfriend named Ken. I know all about them, Barbie Dahl kept me up to date. Her figure, okay Barbie's, the real person Barbie, was in some ways the result of a skilled plastic surgeon, but who cares? I was enjoying myself, and she seemed to like the attention. In fact, she had just rolled on top of me again. I figured it was probably for another close examination of the surgery, but, hey, I was up for it. "You really mean it? Oh what a fun adventure I've never been. God, I'll have to get some new outfits."

An hour later, we were having breakfast. Thankfully, the kitchen wasn't painted Barbie pink the way her bedroom was. Even in the dark, I'd had problems trying to get to sleep. This morning we were eating French toast, I'd made it, and my plate was almost overflowing in maple syrup and butter. Barbie had two bites, proclaimed it exquisite, and then pushed her plate away. Not a problem. Besides, I happen to like French toast, so I placed her plate on top of mine and dug in. Barbie, the doll, apparently weighed one hundred and ten pounds, so Barbie, the real-life hottie, kept her weight there, too, no small feat.

"You mean it? I mean, promise you're not kidding. You'll really take me with you to Vegas?"

"Yeah, it will be fun, if you're sure you want to go. I don't want to force you." I shoveled in another forkful of perfectly done French toast. We were eating off of Barbie plates. She had an even dozen of the things, all pink backgrounds with different headshots of Barbie. The one with my French toast featured Barbie holding a little white dog.

Barbie's little white dog, Sugar, suddenly jumped into her lap and barked across the table at me. Past experience had taught me things seemed to go best if I didn't comment where Sugar was concerned. Barbie reached over and took a piece of French toast from the plate, fed it to Sugar, then licked her fingertips suggestively.

"Mmm-mmm, I haven't been out to Vegas for at least ten years," I said. "There's bound to be something new to see in the place. The people-watching is nothing short of bizarre, not to mention all the games. I learned early on I'm the sort of guy everyone wins money from, so it seems to work best if I don't gamble and just watch. Besides, I could use a couple of days off after working on this latest case. I'm in the process of wrapping it up, so, yeah, the timing is almost perfect."

"Oh, I'm so excited, Dev. This is going to be so much fun. Come on," she said, then stood, dropped her pink silk dressing gown onto the floor, took me by the hand and led me back to her pink bedroom.

Four

ouie shook his head. "Vegas? You gotta be kidding. Didn't you tell me more than once how you hated the place?"

"I do, or, well, at least I did, but then I was never out there with Barbie. This could be a whole new experience. Besides, I'm gonna help out a pal for an hour or two."

We were taking a break across the street at The Spot. Well, at least that had been our original intent when we stopped in for one a little after four. It was almost nine now, and neither one of us was feeling any pain. There was a taco special tonight, and Morton was half-asleep on the floor after devouring a couple of the things.

"By the way, you better give your buddy there a walk before you hit the sack tonight, he ate at least a half-dozen of those things."

"I only bought him three," I said.

"Yeah, but then I bought him three, and that couple sitting at the end of the bar earlier, they gave him another one."

I looked down at Morton. His eyes were closed, and I think he was snoring, although I couldn't be sure with the jukebox playing Bob Seger. Morton had licked the plate clean, and I wanted to make sure Mike remembered to put it in the dishwasher instead of back on the shelf in the kitchen. I reached down and grabbed the thing, your basic white ceramic plate, thank God. Nothing pink and no images of a blonde or that little dog. Just a white plate.

"Mike," I said, placing the plate on the bar. "Toss this in the dishwasher."

"Thing looks clean to me." Then he added, "Relax, just kidding."

"Look, I don't mean to pry," Louie said. "But are you sure you're going to be able to travel out there and spend more than a night together without her strangling you? I mean, I know she's enjoyable on some basic level. But a couple of days, you're liable to drive each other crazy."

"She's never been to the place, Vegas. We'll fly out there, stay for a couple of nights, then head back here while we're still on a high note. I mean, what could go wrong?"

Louie looked at me for a long moment, "In Vegas? Gee, nothing. You gotta be kidding me. Just for starters, if you're going to be paying for this trip, give her cash, not your credit card number. She's liable to . . . What's that look for? You didn't—"

"She wanted to surprise me and book the room."

"Dev, there are places out there that run a thousand, no, tens of thousands a night. She could put you into bankruptcy in about sixty seconds."

"She wouldn't do that, I mean, you don't think she'd…God."

"Report the card as stolen or put a hold on it or something. What the hell were you thinking? On second thought, don't answer that, I already know."

"Maybe I should call her?"

"It might be more productive to simply call your credit card company. I'm guessing they have an 800 number on the back of the card. You can get it straightened out in less than five minutes."

The more I thought about it, the more sense Louie seemed to make. "Mike, give us two more. I gotta step outside and make a phone call."

* * *

Fortunately, there'd been no activity on my card. Far from being financially responsible, I suspected Barbie had just been overwhelmed with the options and couldn't make up her mind. By the time we got home, and I took Morton for a walk, a very good idea, by the way, it was too late to call her. I climbed in bed and immediately fell asleep. My cellphone woke me just before five the following morning.

"Hello," I groaned, trying to sound wide awake and failing miserably. Morton had snuck up onto the bed sometime in the middle of the night. He opened one eye and looked at me for a moment, then angled his head under a pillow, took a deep breath, and went back to sleep. "Hello?"

"Dev?"

"Barbie, is everything okay?"

"I hope I didn't wake you." I glanced at the digital clock on the dresser, four fifty-seven.

"Is everything okay?"

"Well, no, I mean, no big deal. Kind of. I found the perfect place for us to stay in Las Vegas, but when I went to make the reservation, I needed the security code for your credit card."

"Security code?" I said and thought, *'you gotta be kidding me.'*

"Yeah, you know, on the back of the card, should be three little numbers. If you can just give it to me, I'll call them back and make the reservations. I was lucky to find four nights somewhere."

That didn't sound right, the four nights deal. It was the end of July, and the average temperature out in Vegas had to be around a hundred-plus degrees. I mean, the place is always busy, but wouldn't the hot summer be something like an off-season?

"Hello, are you there? Can you give me those numbers on the back of your card?"

"Yeah, I suppose, hang on, and I'll grab it." My wallet was on the dresser, right next to the digital that now read four fifty-nine. Fortunately, I'd come awake enough to walk down the hall to the bathroom, then back into the bedroom. "You still there?"

"Yeah, what kept you?"

"I was looking for my credit card. It's not in my wallet," I lied. "It's either at the restaurant where I was in a meeting last night, or I left it at the office."

"Mmm-mmm," she said, not sounding too surprised. "Could you call the restaurant and see? Maybe they could give you the security numbers thingy."

"I don't think anyone will be there at this hour. How about I call you when I have it in my hand?"

"You won't forget?"

"No, I won't forget," I said, and jealousy looked over at Morton, sound asleep with his head buried beneath the pillow.

"Promise?"

I was almost back asleep myself, and I half-groaned, "I promise."

"Okay, call me just as soon as you get it. Bye, bye, bye, bye, bye," she said, sounding all cheery as she hung up.

I switched my cellphone into airplane mode, tossed it on the bedside table, then tried to get comfortable in the little bit of room that Morton had left me. I slept fitfully for the next few hours before I finally got up, stumbled downstairs, and made some coffee. Morton came into the kitchen about an hour later, gave a long stretch, and then waited for me by the back door until I let him out.

I went online, looking for an inexpensive room in Vegas while at the same time trying to figure out how I would explain it to Barbie.

Five

We were having a coffee at the Claddagh coffee shop down on West Seventh. People at the tables on either side of us looked over for a moment before returning to their conversations.

"You already made the reservations?" Barbie half-screamed.

"Yeah, and I got a pretty good deal. It's a Holiday Inn and—"

"A Holiday Inn?" she said just a little louder than her previous scream.

"Yeah, it's in south Vegas."

"Does that mean it's on the strip?"

"The strip? Well, no, not exactly. See, that's why I got such a good deal. You wanted to be on the strip?"

"God, Dev!" This time when she screamed, there was no 'half' about it.

The woman from behind the cash register walked over and asked, "Is everything all right?"

"Yeah, fine," I said.

"Fine! Are you kidding me?" Barbie looked at the woman for sympathy, "No, it's horrible. We're going to

Las Vegas, supposedly for fun, but certain people booked us into a Holiday Inn outside of town."

"Why aren't you staying on the strip?" the woman asked me, then turned and looked at Barbie. "We go out there every year. We always stay at the Bellagio. They've got a great buffet, a wonderful little piano bar where we people-watch, and it has that famous fountain out in front, everybody knows about the Bellagio." She looked down at me and smiled, suggesting I was a no-body and didn't know. "I just love to play the games. I always win."

I doubted that and was about to say something when Barbie's withering glance convinced me it might be better to just remain quiet. "The Bellagio," Barbie said, then looked at me with raised eyebrows.

Six

She was wearing a sexy little white skirt with a pink top that basically exposed her entire cleavage and then some. I had been trying to figure out how she kept them from bouncing out but thought it might be the better idea to keep that question to myself and just enjoy the view. I guessed she'd be one of the few women, if not the only one, wearing six-inch stiletto heels on the flight. We'd already dropped Morton off in his kennel for the flight. He'd just cast a disdainful look in my direction, then turned his back on me.

Sugar was prancing around on the end of a pink leash while we checked in. I thought about drop-kicking her over the customer service counter but decided against it.

"Are you checking any bags?" the woman in the Delta uniform on the other side of the counter asked.

"Yes, just these two," Barbie said as I hoisted the first one onto the scale next to the counter. It was large, pink, weighed a ton, and I half-groaned when I lifted it.

"Oh, my," the woman said, then looked at the two of us for a long moment until the claim check was printed off. She pulled the backing off the end, wrapped it around the handle on the suitcase, sent it down the conveyer, then stuck the little receipt with the tracking number onto Barbie's boarding pass.

I hoisted the second suitcase onto the scale. It was a matching bright pink and even heavier than the first one. The woman read the digital read-off on the scale, then looked from me to Barbie, then back to me again. "How long are you going to be gone?"

"Four whole nights," Barbie said, then flashed a smile.

"That will be seventy-five dollars for the suitcase. They're, umm, pretty heavy."

"That's okay," Barbie said.

"Seventy-five bucks?" I said.

"Yes, sir, that's for each, so one-fifty total. We take Visa or American Express," she smiled, suggesting I was somehow getting the deal of a lifetime.

"Dev," Barbie cautioned.

* * *

I was drinking a glass of cran-apple, looking out the window at what passed for scenery down below. It was all reddish sand that reminded me of an awful lot of construction rubble. There was no sign of human habitation, not even so much as a road. Barbie was having a glass of white wine, and at the moment, Sugar was curled up on her lap. Occasionally, the dog would stand on its hind legs, and shoot a quick glance my way before she licked

Barbie's cleavage, only because she could. Then she'd curl back up on her lap so Barbie could feed her one of the pretzels from the little sample bag the flight attendant had passed out to me.

"Are you going to be Mr. Crabby the entire time we're out here?"

"Barbie, a hundred and fifty bucks for your two suitcases. We're only going to be in Vegas for a couple of days, and the average temperature will be somewhere north of a hundred degrees the entire time. All you need is a pair of shorts and some flip-flops."

"That's your idea of a fun time? Gee, hopefully, we'll be close to a McDonalds, and we can just eat there every day. For your information, Mister, I intend to enjoy myself. Now, if you're going to be a party pooper, you can always sleep on the couch."

"The couch?"

"Yes, in the living room. The room I booked for us at the Bellagio has a living room, three bathrooms, and a gorgeous super Caesar king-sized bed. Where just about anything you can possibly imagine could happen, Dev, provided certain people start wearing a smile," she said, then rubbed my arm.

"Okay, okay. It's just that the hundred and fifty bucks for your suitcases maybe caught me a little off guard, is all. I mean, you got that big bag I stored overhead, I thought you packed everything in that. I'm traveling with one suitcase, and it's half-full of your stuff."

"Oh, that's right, Dev, I want to dress like you, that'll be attractive, not. I might as well hold a cardboard sign that says 'homeless and boring.' Oh, and, by the way, your suitcase, the one with the duct tape along the side and the paint splattered across it, no, I have standards, after all. Besides, that big bag you stored overhead just holds my makeup. Which reminds me, we're going to have to stop somewhere so I can get my creams. That TSA guy confiscated all of them, probably going to bring them home to his wife tonight."

"Three ounces is the TSA guideline."

"For creams? Come on, those were really expensive. Besides, do I look like some kind of terrorist?"

I had to agree with her there.

"That's better, a smile. Here, you take Sugar. I'm running to the loo." With that, she drained her glass, set it on my table, then handed her little white dog to me. As I grabbed the thing, it sort of growled at me, and I thought, *I've eaten sandwiches bigger than you.*

Seven

We landed on time, then waited about thirty minutes for the plane to empty before we could get out of our seats. Barbie finally stood up, then headed down the aisle carrying Sugar. I pulled my suitcase out of the overhead bin, then grabbed her makeup bag, a shiny black thing large enough to hold a small child, and followed.

Her bright pink suitcases were easy enough to spot amidst all the luggage in the baggage claim area. But getting the two of them, plus my suitcase with the paint splatter and duct tape, plus the makeup bag, all to the taxi stand was another matter, somehow I managed to make it. I took Morton for a brisk ten-minute walk to get him somewhat calmed down after the flight. He was just thankful to be rescued from the kennel he'd been confined to and behaved perfectly.

"Where to, folks?" the taxi driver asked as he got out of the taxi and lifted the lid to the trunk.

"Bellagio," Barbie smiled, then climbed in the back seat of the taxi and sat there exchanging kisses with Sugar. It was a fifteen-minute ride that ran twenty-five bucks with the tip. All in all, I figured that was fair. We made our way through one of three revolving doors at the Bellagio and checked in. Surprise, surprise, they charged us an additional fee for Morton and Sugar, plus a damage deposit of twelve hundred dollars on the suite, refundable at checkout time provided there wasn't any damage. We made our way up to the suite on the thirty-sixth floor. Thankfully with all the luggage and two dogs, we were the only ones in the elevator. We stepped off the elevator, and Goose was standing there in a red blazer with an earphone attached to his ear. As the elevator door opened, he pasted a surprised look on his face and said, "Dev? Dev Haskell?"

I turned, pretended to act just as surprised, and said, "Goose? Goose Gander?"

"What are you doing in Vegas?" he asked, then he focused in on Barbie and her cleavage. "Well, hello there. I'm Goose, I can get you anything you'd like." He held out his hand, and when Barbie extended hers, he took it and kissed it.

"Goose and I played hockey together in high school. Gee, you're working out here, man, who knew?" I said, nodding at his red blazer and the white earphone.

"Yeah, small world, isn't it? Hey, where's your room? Let me help you with some of this stuff. Who's this guy?" he asked, bending down. He gave Morton a rub behind the ears, which sent Morton's tail wagging and bouncing off the wall.

"That's Morton."

"And this is Sugar," Barbie said, holding her sixteen-ounce dog out in Goose's direction.

"Pleased to meet both of you," he said and stared at Barbie for a long moment. "Hey, come on, what's the room number? I'll give you a hand." With that, he headed down the hall toward our room before I'd even given him the room number, pulling the two pink suitcases behind him.

"Thirty-six-oh-two-five, " I said, looking at the small folder with the two credit card keys. Morton surged ahead, trying to catch up to Goose.

We passed two rooms, and Goose stopped at the third. He slipped a master key into the door, and it clicked open. "Here we go, home sweet home," he said, walking into the spacious suite. To say it was elegant was an understatement.

"Oh my God, this is gorgeous," Barbie said as she and Sugar hurried past me.

I was sort of in shock and just stood there staring with my mouth hanging open. There was a large living room with three plush couches, and a gigantic flat screen mounted on the wall. A bar with four stools curved out from a far corner. Next to the bar, a sliding glass door that opened out onto a balcony.

"Man, you must be doing pretty damn good," Goose whispered to me as Barbie opened the door to the balcony and stepped outside.

"They just took my credit card info but were kind of light on the details at the front desk. Barbie made the reservation. What's this joint run a night?"

Goose looked at me and snickered, then rubbed his index finger and thumb together. "You kidding me, man? If you have to ask that, you can't afford this place."

I gave him a shocked look just as Barbie stepped back into the room. "It's gotta be about a thousand degrees out there."

"Actually, it's only a hundred and twelve right now, but it'll heat up as the afternoon goes on. Of course, it's a dry heat," Goose said.

"Yeah, so is my oven, but I don't stick my head in it," I replied.

Barbie stepped behind the bar and opened the refrigerator. "Oh, isn't this sweet. Look, Dev, a bottle of wine and a card," she opened the small envelope and began to read aloud. "'*Thank you for being our guest. Enjoy your stay.*' Now isn't that nice. Don't mind if I do," she said, then took a wine glass from behind the bar, twisted the cap off the bottle and poured herself a glass.

"They did tell you about the refrigerator, didn't they? When you checked in."

"Huh?"

"The bottle of wine Barbie opened is on the house," Goose said. "Kind of shit wine, if you ask me," he added under his breath. "The fridge works on weight, so if you remove a bottle or a can from there for more than sixty seconds, they automatically charge it to your room bill."

"You're kidding," I said.

"Cool," Barbie said. She took a sip of wine, made a funny sort of face, then stepped from behind the bar, wandered past us and into the bedroom. "Oh. My. God."

Goose smiled and gave me the thumbs-up.

"Dev, you have got to see this. Get in here."

"Be there in just a minute. I'm unloading all of your luggage." I followed Goose into the room. Another large flat screen was mounted on the wall opposite the deluxe, super Caesar king-sized bed. There were six big, fluffy pillows on the bed. The ceiling in the room was painted to look like blue sky and clouds. Morton and Sugar hurried past, jumped up onto the bed, and settled in with both of them wearing looks like they were just waiting for me to try and move them off the bed. There was another mini bar on the far side of the bed with two stools. A vase holding a large bouquet of flowers sat on the end of the bar. Barbie opened a small envelope leaning against the vase.

"Hope you enjoy your stay, Mr. Haskell. So happy you chose the Bellagio," Barbie read, then looked up at me. "My God, Dev, you're some big-time guy out here. Why didn't you tell me?" she said, then tossed the card back on the bar and wrapped her arms around my neck. "Oh, believe me, you are *so* going to enjoy this."

Goose pointed to himself with his thumb indicating he'd sent the flowers, then fluttered his tongue in and out while Barbie hugged me.

"Oh, gee, Goose. I guess we better let you get back to work. What time is your shift over?"

"I'm finished at seven. How 'bout we meet for one beer at the piano bar down off the lobby, then I'll let you two get back to doing whatever naughty behavior you planned on for the rest of the night. Okay?"

"Perfect, that will give us some time to get settled in here," I smiled.

Barbie sort of ran her hand across my shoulder a couple of times, then kissed my cheek.

"See you, Goose."

"I'll let myself out so you can… get settled," he said, then hurried out of the bedroom.

Barbie waited until we heard the door close, then said, "Dev, oh my God. You never told me you had connections out here. God, they…"

"Goose? I told you, we played hockey together in high school."

"Not Goose, silly. The flowers, that doesn't just happen to everyone. That's really big."

"No, it's just…"

"Come on, stand over there next to the flowers. I want to take your picture."

"Don't take my picture. We can…"

"Stand over there next to the flowers. I'm taking your picture, and if you behave and smile, then we can try out the bed."

I hurried over to the flowers and gave a big grin.

"There, much better. Okay, you two, you're in the way, go on out to the other room," Barbie said, shooing both dogs off the bed and into the living room. She closed the door behind them, then turned toward me and began to slowly unzip her white skirt. "Let's try the bed out and see if you like it."

"I think that's a pretty safe bet I will."

Eight

Apparently, we dozed off. I glanced at the digital clock on the bedside table, twenty after six. I blinked and rotated my shoulders before I rolled over to wake Barbie. Instead, I looked into Morton's brown eyes. He licked my face a couple of times, which I guess was nice, although not exactly what I had been expecting.

Barbie called me a moment later from the bathroom. "Dev, time to get up, we're supposed to meet that Goose person at seven. Dev, are you awake?"

I had to clear my throat a couple of times, then rolled out of bed and walked to the bathroom. Barbie was seated on a small stool with a white towel wrapped around her waist. She was in the process of applying eye makeup and looking into an oval-shaped mirror with a light around it. The mirror was resting on a marble vanity top. Sugar was sitting on the floor next to the Jacuzzi staring attentively at her topless master. The Jacuzzi sported the remnants of a bubble bath.

"You went into the Jacuzzi without me?"

"We deal with our afternoon delights a little differently. I, on the one hand, thought a warm Jacuzzi with a fragrant bubble bath might be just the frosting on the cake. You, on the other hand, just rolled over and started to snore. I thought it best to escape from your snoring in here if only to hold onto what was left of my sanity."

"Oh, sorry about that."

She remained focused on her image in the makeup mirror. At the moment, her tool of choice was a little mascara brush. She half-laughed and said, "Actually, it was sort of nice to stretch out and have the thing all to myself. Not that we won't enjoy it together at some point."

"I woke up next to Morton."

"How special," she said, meaning anything but, then she straightened up, blinked a couple of times, and looked at me. "What are you wearing this evening?"

"Wearing? I don't know, jeans and a t-shirt, I guess. I'm was thinking we could grab something at that pancake joint we passed on the way in, it's open twenty-four hours and…"

"I'd say you're kidding, but, unfortunately, I know better. No, Dev darling. We are not going to eat at that *pancake joint.*' And, let me save you the trouble, we're not going to eat at a McDonalds, a Burger King, or a Kentucky Fried Chicken. I've worked up an appetite, thanks to you," she raised her eyebrows. "And you are going to wine and dine me. Now, we're going to meet with this Goose person." She stood, dropped the towel onto the stool, and grabbed a pink thong from the marble vanity top. She stretched the thong between her two index fingers while I took in the view. "I'm sure your friend can direct us to somewhere I'll enjoy. We will meet him for one, and no more than two drinks, and then you will be able to spend the remainder of the night wining, dining, and entertaining me."

"All I brought were jeans and a couple of t-shirts."

"Why am I not surprised? We'll address that soon enough. Right now, you should hit the shower. We have to be down at that piano bar in twenty-five minutes. Oh, and you have my lipstick on your back. You may want to scrub that off."

"I may want to keep it as a souvenir and show Goose."

"You could do that, and then just leave it on forever, because it would be the last time it ever happened."

"I'll scrub it off in the shower."

Nine

We were on our third round at the piano bar. Goose and I were drinking beer. Barbie was sucking down pina coladas through a straw, mesmerized by the throngs of people strolling past and completely ignoring Goose and me. Sugar was curled up on her lap.

I didn't mention it, but my jeans and a clean t-shirt appeared to be on the upper end of a fashion statement for ninety-nine percent of the guys. The women were a different story, everything from thong bikinis on tanned bodies, to soccer moms in plaid shorts and hot looking women dressed to the nines for a night out on the Vegas strip.

"I've seen them over at The Palms a couple of times. They're always together, the three of them, usually at one of the craps tables." Goose had been filling me in on the three guys who'd been trying to get chummy with his brother, Kenny.

"Are they playing, gambling?"

"Occasionally, but not so you'd notice. I mean, they don't bet huge amounts. Usually, one of them will just toss out a dollar chip and play that. If they lose, they don't bet another one. If they win, they'll play a couple more times, like they're maybe trying to learn the game. The only thing is, they're not tourists, I think they live here."

"You know where?"

He shook his head no. "I've asked some of the guys. It's always the same answer. They look familiar, but no one knows who the hell they are. I know they're up to something, I just don't know what and I sure as hell don't want Kenny mixed up in anything."

"How do they even know about Kenny?"

"That's another question I have. I told you he works at The Palms, but he's, like, in the accounting office or a closet someplace, it's not like he's out wandering the floor. He's working off computer print offs, looking at numbers all day. They've got him going over percentages and betting trends and stuff. He's in his element. I think statistics, mostly. It's not like he's numbering cards or balancing roulette wheels or something. And Kenny wouldn't be involved in anything illegal, anyway, he's not wired like that. My concern is he's so innocent and trusting that, well, these guys could get hold of him, and he's so damn vulnerable. I'm just worried about him."

"Hey, Goose, honey, point me toward the ladies' room," Barbie said, then took a long sip on the straw until her glass was drained before she set it on the table.

"See where that woman is over there in the blue outfit?" Goose said and pointed across the way.

Barbie looked past the crowd of people flowing by toward a woman in a sparkly blue cocktail dress that barely covered her essentials. The dress seemed to hang loosely from her shoulders down. She wore silver, open-toe shoes with about a six-inch heel that forced her into a funny sort of walk, not quite straightening her leg when she stepped.

"I think that's a Sherry Hill," Barbie said.

"You know her?"

"Her dress, silly, the designer is Sherry Hill," she said, sounding like that was supposed to mean something to me. "I wonder if they have that in pink…"

"Just follow that woman around the edge of the room, and you'll come to the ladies' room. If you get to the sushi restaurant, you've gone about fifteen feet too far," Goose said.

"Okay, thanks, back in a minute. Order me another, Dev," she said as she stood.

"I thought you just wanted to have— I'll have it waiting for you by the time you get back," I said in response to the look she gave me.

Goose watched her walk down the three steps from the piano bar to the main floor with Sugar tucked under her arm. She made her way across the non-stop foot traffic to the less traveled carpet along the edge of the casino, then followed it toward the ladies' room.

"I gotta tell you, Dev. She's really something. God, she reminds me of someone, but I can't quite put my finger on who. Maybe someone from high school or—"

"Barbie."

"What?"

"Barbie, that doll all the girls had when we were kids. In fact, I think they still have them. She's Barbie. She's obsessed with the thing. Knows all this stuff, what kind of car Barbie has, that dog of her's."

"Sugar?"

"Yeah, it's named after Barbie's dog. The plates in her kitchen all have an image of Barbie. She's always wearing something pink."

"What are you talking about? She's in that sexy black dress. God, you catch all the guys giving her the eye as they walked past?"

"Her thong is pink."

"Thanks for sharing."

"Her bedroom is all pink. Her suitcases are pink. You saw them, in fact, you had to drag them into our room. I tell you, I thought I was going to have a heart attack just getting all that stuff onto the elevator."

"Not to mention your dogs."

"Don't even go there. Hey, thanks for the flowers, by the way, she thinks I'm connected."

"Well, I really appreciate you coming out here to check on Kenny. Besides, I probably never would have met Barbie if you hadn't brought her along. I just saw those flowers waiting to be delivered to your room, so I brought them up."

"What? I thought you bought them."

"Me? Buy flowers for you, are you nuts? No, some-one sent them, I just figured it was you trying to impress Barbie."

Tubby Gustafson came immediately to mind. I didn't say anything to Goose. Right now, I wasn't sure who I could trust.

"Speaking of Barbie, I better order that drink for her. You up for another beer?"

Ten

We finished our beers, the fresh ones, and Barbie still hadn't returned from the ladies' room. By this time, her pina colada had warmed to room temperature. The ingredients had separated in the glass, leaving about an inch of a sort of golden-colored liquid on the bottom of the glass and a milky white substance the rest of the way up.

"I wonder if she took a wrong turn coming out of the ladies' room?" I said. "She was hiding behind the door when they were passing out any sense of direction. She's always getting lost, even in places she should be familiar with."

"This casino looks big, but it ain't that big. As long as she doesn't go out any doors or onto an elevator, she should be pretty easy to find. Hang on for a second, let me make a call and have them scout around for her." Goose pulled out his cellphone and hit some speed-dial number.

"Yeah, Jerry? Goose. Hey, I'm with a pal, his girlfriend headed off to the ladies' room about an hour ago and hasn't come back. Yeah, right, very funny. No. Listen. She's a hot looking blonde," Goose nodded in my direction. "Nice rack, in a short black dress with spaghetti straps, black heels with straps around the ankles and sparkly little buckles. Oh, and she's carrying a little white dog. You are? Yeah, I know, that's her real name, and I just learned she's really into the whole thing. No, I just met her this afternoon. She's with my pal. They're out here from Minnesota. Yeah, I'll be sure to pass that along, not. Which table? Five, got it, we'll be there in a couple of minutes. Thanks, man."

"So?"

"They've been watching her. Don't take offense, but they thought she might be a high priced working girl. She's over at one of the craps tables, come on, we'll go get her and bring her back."

"What the hell is she doing at a craps table?"

"Just watching, at least for the moment. If I might make a suggestion?"

"Go ahead."

"Get a couple of chips for her and let her make some field bets. They pay out three-to-one, so it looks great, but the odds to win are worse than fifty-fifty, she'll lose all her chips, get depressed, and she'll be cured forever. It might cost you fifty bucks, but once she's against gambling at the craps table, you'll be ahead of the game. Way ahead."

"You sure?"

"I've seen it work a thousand times on any given day. Believe me, she won't win betting the field, and once she gets it in her head that she's gonna lose, that's just where you want her to be. I mean, look at this place, Dev. You think they got all this glitz around here because everyone is winning all the time?"

"Sounds like a plan," I said.

Goose walked me over to a cashier's window. "Give him a hundred bucks in five dollar chips, Marlene. Charge it to thirty-six-oh-two-five," Goose said.

"A hundred bucks? I thought you said fifty."

"Yeah, Dev, fifty for the craps table, but once she loses at craps, then she's going to want to play roulette, have her bet on a number, any number on roulette, she'll never win. Then she'll want to try blackjack and end up just getting spanked. Believe me, for a hundred bucks, you're getting off easy, man. Folks lose their houses and businesses every day out here. I'm telling you, it's just crazy."

"A hundred bucks, this better work, Goose."

"Trust me," he said.

Eleven

We found Barbie focused on the craps table. There were maybe five people standing around the table, we arrived just as some guy rolled the dice, and everyone groaned except for the guy who threw the dice.

He half-shouted, "God damn it," then picked up both his chips and stormed away. The crowd quickly dwindled down to Barbie, Goose, me, and some guy in a wrinkled pinstripe suit who looked like he'd been up for seventy-two hours.

"Oh, here you are, Barbie, we were beginning to worry about you."

She looked at me with glazed eyes and said, "I'm feeling really lucky."

Goose stood behind her and nodded at me.

"Oh, good, I figured you might be. Hey, look, I got some chips for you, here," I said, then poured the twenty, red, five-dollar chips into her cupped hands.

"What? Oh, I love you, Dev, this is just fantastic. Thank you, thank you," she said and quickly spun around to face the table. She arranged the chips into two neat stacks of ten red chips each, then placed both stacks in an area marked 2-12.

"Barbie, do you think you should do that, I mean, bet all your chips? Honey, that's a hundred bucks you just bet."

"Huh? I just set them there. I just want to bet one at a time. A hundred dollars? Is that why they're a different color? I thought each one was worth a dollar."

"The white ones are a dollar, those red ones are five bucks. Each!"

Goose stood behind her shaking his head at me.

"I don't want to bet all of that on…" she said just as the guy in the wrinkled suit tossed the dice, and they bounced off the far corner.

"And the lady wins at three to one," the stickman (actually a woman) said. She had this cane sort of thing, and she raked in all the chips on the table except for Barbie's. The guy in the wrinkled pinstripe suit shot a quick look at Barbie and grabbed the dice. One of the cashiers tossed three black chips next to Barbie's stacks.

"I won, I won, oh, that's so great!" She hopped up and down, and in the process, getting the attention of the guy in the wrinkled pinstripe, one of the cashiers and Goose, all of whom just stared. "Look, Dev, I won fifteen dollars, and I didn't even mean to."

"No, honey, you just won three hundred dollars. Those chips they gave you, the black ones, they're worth a hundred bucks each."

"Place your bets folks, place your bets," the stick-man said as she cast an eye toward Barbie.

"The red ones you have are worth five bucks each and the…"

"So I've tripled our money in just one little minute! Oh, this is so exciting," she squealed and clapped her hands just as wrinkled pinstripe tossed the dice again.

"The black ones are each worth a hundred bucks," I reminded her.

"What should I bet next?" Barbie asked, just as the dice came to a rest.

"You already did, honey, you better start paying attention."

"What?" she screamed as the stickman raked in all the chips except hers. She tossed two purple and two black chips onto Barbie's pile of chips. Barbie gave me a questioning look, and I looked over at Goose for help.

"You just won twelve hundred bucks, honey," Goose said, shaking his head. "The purple chips are five hundred each. The black are a hundred."

"Woo-hoo-hoo," Barbie screamed as she jumped up and down again. People started to drift over to the table, but I couldn't tell if they were interested in the betting or just watching Barbie jump up and down.

"Place your bets, folks, place your bets."

"Oh. My. God. What should I do, Dev? What should I do?"

"Take your chips off the table before you lose everything."

"I can't. I'm still feeling lucky. You saw it. You saw how lucky I was. Weren't you watching?"

"Place your bets, folks. Place your bets," the stickman said, then shot a glance at Barbie before she slowly began to push the dice toward wrinkled pinstripe.

"Oh, oh," Barbie groaned.

"Get the damn chips off the table. You've got fifteen hundred bucks there, don't be stupid."

At the word, 'stupid' Barbie shot me a look, then curled her lower lip and pushed the entire pile of chips onto the number three, looked at me, and said, "There, happy? We'll just see who's stupid."

"What the hell are you doing?" I said as wrinkled pinstripe snatched up the dice and shook them in his hand.

"Three, for March," Barbie said.

"What?" I asked just as the dice were thrown.

"March, the third month, Dev. As in three. Barbie's birthday is in March, well, and mine too. The same day, March ninth. Hello."

"Three," the stickman shouted as claps and cheers erupted from the crowd.

"Jesus Christ, that pays fifteen to one," Goose said as one of the cashiers began to count out twenty-two thousand five hundred dollars in chips. He made two tall stacks of twenty chips each, a smaller stack of five chips, and pushed them all toward Barbie's pile sitting on the number three.

"Come on, you're cashing out a winner," I said and reached for her chips.

"No, Dev, don't," Barbie said and roughly pushed me back.

"Sir, please, or I'll have to call security," the stick-man said, then shot a look at Goose.

"She means it, Dev. Those chips are Barbie's winnings. She can do whatever she wants with them."

"Yeah, so there. And I'm betting it all on the number nine," Barbie said, pushing a small stack across the table toward the number nine. "Our birthday, for your information, Barbie and me. Our lucky birthday," she said and stuck her tongue out at me. "Go ahead, honey, roll 'em," she said to wrinkled pinstripe.

It seemed to take forever, but it couldn't have been more than a second or two.

"Nine!" the stickman shouted with a shocked look on her face. A cheer went up from the crowd, now easily ten deep standing around the table.

"Ooooh," Barbie squealed and looked at Goose. "This is really fun. How much is that?"

"I think it pays thirty-five to one," Goose said.

"Hmm-mmm, should have bet more chips."

"Honey, you won close to fifty grand in about the last ten minutes. Can we just take this back to the room and maybe rest for a little bit?"

"I have a better idea, how 'bout a Pina Colada?"

"Yeah, sure, good idea, can I pick up your chips, please? So we can get out of here."

"Place your bets, place your bets."

"We're cashing out," I said. One of the cashiers took out a tray, quickly lined up Barbie's chips in the tray then handed it across the table to her.

"Don't forget to leave them a tip," Goose whispered. "And you should give one to that guy who was throwing the dice, too. Looks like he could use it."

Twelve

e were walking back to the piano bar. Big spender Barbie had just promised the first round was on her. People were actually stopping to applaud as she walked past carrying her tray of chips.

Some guy called out, "I'm cheap, easy, and available."

Goose leaned over and half-whispered to me, "Hey, you see that?"

"That guy? He didn't mean anything by it. He was just joking."

"Not him, idiot, our friends."

"Friends?"

"Don't look now, but our three friends are following us."

"You sure?" I said and half-turned to look.

"Hey, did you hear what I just said? What the hell do you think you're doing? Don't let them know we recognize them. And you're the P.I.? Get a grip, Dev. Yeah, didn't you see them before? They were in that crowd of folks watching Barbie win."

"Oh, yeah," I lied. "Three of them, right? I thought it might be them, but I wasn't sure. And plus, I was trying to get Barbie out of there before she lost it all. Great plan, by the way. I'm sure she's really off of gambling now. Thanks."

"Yeah, sorry 'bout that. Who knew she was so lucky?"

"Well, she caught me."

"Yeah, like I said, who knew she was lucky. Anyway, this is great. I didn't know how I was going to get you hooked up with these guys. Looks like 'Little Miss Lucky' went and got it all arranged on her own. Hopefully, they'll head into the piano bar. I think it might be a good idea if we have security escort you two up to your room tonight. Be an even better idea if she cashed in those chips before too long."

"Let's get a drink in her, and maybe she'll calm down. God, I'm sure now she'll want to stay at the craps table for as long as we're out here and sleep on the plane on the way home."

"Well, I'm not wishing her any bad luck, but they can lose it even faster than she won it. I've seen it happen out here too many times."

We were at the entrance to the piano bar, Barbie went up the three steps carrying her tray of chips like it was a gift ready to be presented to the Queen, which, in a way, I guess it was.

The receptionist eyed the tray, then pasted a wide smile on her face and said, "Would you prefer a table out here, ma'am, or something inside where it's more quiet and private?"

"Hmm-mmm, I think out here where I can watch everyone walk by."

"Oh, I know what you mean, the people-watching is just fabulous, isn't it?"

Barbie nodded, and Goose and I followed. I gave a casual glance to the crowd of passersby and thought I picked up the three guys Goose had mentioned. They seemed to be hanging back by a bank of slot machines. Our server arrived before I'd sat down.

"I'll have one of our snack trays for you in just a moment," she said, then placed a menu in front of each of us. "Specials tonight on beer until midnight, gentlemen. Do you know what you'd like to drink? Or do you need a couple of minutes?"

"I'll have a pina colada," Barbie said.

"Excellent choice, ma'am."

"Sir," she said to Goose, then gave him a funny sort of look.

"Hi, Carol, it's me, Goose. I'll have a beer, make it a bottle of that Torpedo Extra IPA."

"Sure, Goose. Sir, something from the bar?"

"What do you have on tap?"

"Actually, nothing. It's all in bottles."

"Then I'll have what Goose is having."

"I'll be back with your drinks in just a minute," she said and left. I noticed the three guys I'd caught sight of a moment ago had just walked to the far side of the piano and sat down at a table.

Barbie set her tray of chips on the table, then gave Sugar a hug and a kiss. "Oooooh, Mommy is a very lucky lady tonight. I can't believe we won all this, baby. How much did you say it was?" she said and looked at me.

"Almost fifty grand," Goose replied. "If you don't mind me giving you some advice, after these drinks, we should probably go to a cashier's window and cash all of this in. Walking around with that tray of chips, you might as well tape a bunch of hundred dollar bills to your dress and mingle with the crowd."

"Oh, but it was so much fun! Here, want to touch them?" she said and pushed the tray toward Goose.

He paused for a moment, then said, "The chips? No, thanks, Barbie, I've seen enough of them out here. You were lucky. Very lucky, and that usually doesn't happen. Don't think it will happen again, because it just doesn't. If you were smart, as much as it pains me, I have to agree with Dev. You should listen to him on this. Amazingly, he's right. Once we're finished here, you should cash those chips in for safekeeping. That's a really tempting offer you're carrying around there. It wouldn't take much for some crazy to run past, and in a split second, grab a handful then take off out the door. It's unfortunate, but once in awhile, the wrong sort of person will see what you've won and take a chance at grabbing some for himself."

"He's right, Barbie. Be a shame to lose all that after you worked so hard to get it."

Carol arrived with the drinks, two bottles of beer, and a pina colada, plus a little tray of snacks that consisted of chips and nuts. "I'm buying," Barbie said, then placed a hundred dollar chip on Carol's drink tray.

"She can take that as a tip," Goose said. "But you have to pay with cash, credit card, or charge it to your room.

"Okay," Barbie said, "Thirty-six-oh-two-five is our room number, and that can just be your tip."

"Thank you," Carol said and hurried away.

"You know you just gave her a hundred dollar tip," I said.

"What?" Barbie screamed. "I thought that was the five-dollar chip."

"I think after these drinks Goose and I better escort you over to the cashier and get those chips cashed in while you still have them."

Barbie took a long sip from her pina colada through a straw. Just as I was starting to wonder when she'd come up for air, she let go of the straw and said, "Okay. I guess you're probably right. I still have to pinch myself just to see if this really happened. I wonder if I'd be as lucky at another table?"

Goose shot me a look.

"It might be a good idea if you quit while you're ahead. You know, end on a high note, and—"

"But I still feel lucky, Dev," she said. She shrugged her shoulders, wrinkled her nose at me, and I knew I was toast.

Thirteen

Goose checked out about a quarter to one and went home to bed. I followed Barbie around to three different craps tables before she ended up at the same table where she made her big score earlier in the evening. She continued to win, but nowhere near what she'd done earlier in the evening. The three guys who followed us into the piano bar were always within sight yet kept some distance. They took individual turns watching Barbie at the different craps tables but never did anything remotely out of line. Just casual tourists, like us, looking around. I couldn't figure out what they were up to, and at half-past three, I had neither the energy nor the desire to find out.

Some red-headed woman in khaki shorts with a brown leather purse slung over her shoulder, and a black t-shirt that read '*Proud to be a bitch*' had just rolled the dice. However they came up, Barbie lost, again. I was fighting to keep my eyes open.

"Hey, you about ready to head up to the room? I'm starting to fall asleep standing up." I was holding Sugar, who was already asleep in my arms.

"Yeah, I guess so. I think my luck has cooled off a little from before," she said just as the stickman raked two of her five-dollar chips away.

"Might be a good time to quit for the night."

"I suppose," she said, sounding disappointed.

"Barbie, you're still cashing out a winner, a big winner. How much are you up?"

"Not that much, I think it's only about a hundred dollars since we started again and," she looked at her watch. "I've been at this for five hours."

"That evens out to something like twenty bucks an hour, and you've been having fun, that ain't all bad. Besides, Goose got you to cash in all those other chips, what was the receipt for? Forty-six thousand five hundred dollars? Not a bad day's work, Barbie. It's more than just about anyone else has ever made."

"Certainly more than I ever made in a day. In fact, more than I've made in a number of different years."

"Yeah, so what do you say we just head off to bed? I'll even throw in a back rub."

"That's a deal, one more bet, and we leave. Okay?"

"One more," I said, then gave her a look that suggested I really meant it. She placed two chips on the number three, and my first thought was, *here we go again.*

Fortunately, she lost, and as the stickman raked in her chips, Barbie turned to me and said, "How 'bout that back rub?"

We made our way through the casino, then took a left and headed toward the bank of elevators. As we turned, I saw the three guys hanging back but still following. There was a security guard at the elevators, and we had to show him our room key. He gave a polite nod, and we walked to the elevators labeled 32-39. I had to insert my room key in the elevator before I could push the button for our floor. Three minutes later, I was pushing the 'Do Not Disturb' button next to the door of our room. Barbie walked past me, dropped a pile of chips on the table, then opened her handbag and dumped a bunch of chips, a lipstick, a makeup container, a tube of cream, and the keys for her car sitting back in Minnesota onto the table. She sat down in a chair and unbuckled the little strap around her ankles, then kicked off her shoes.

"God, that feels a lot better."

I handed little sleeping Sugar to her, then opened the bedroom door to check on Morton. He was asleep on the bed, nestled into a large pile of feathers from the two pillows he had destroyed. Feathers were scattered across the floor from one end of the room to the other.

"Morton, what the hell did you do?"

He half-opened his eyes, sort of blew the feathers away from his nose, then closed his eyes, took a deep breath, and went back to sleep.

"What's wrong?" Barbie said.

"Morton. The idiot destroyed two pillows, and the bedroom is about knee-deep in feathers."

"I'm too tired to care," Barbie said, then walked past me carrying Sugar, placed her on one of the remaining pillows on the bed, and said, "Unzip me, will you Dev?" I immediately thought *'what a perfect end to a long night.'* I slowly pulled the zipper down the back of her dress as I snuggled against the back of her neck and began to kiss her.

"Mmm-mmm, that's really nice," she said, letting her dress drop to the floor. "Why don't you take that other pillow, it'll make the couch more comfortable."

"The couch?"

"Dev, it's almost five in the morning. I'm tired, Morton and Sugar are already asleep, and I don't want to wake them. Take the couch, and you can give me that back rub in the morning."

"Maybe just a little…"

"Good night, Dev. See you in the morning," she said, then tossed the pillow at me and hustled me out of the bedroom. A trail of feathers followed me out to one of the couches in the living room.

Fourteen

A poke from Morton's cold nose woke me a few hours later. "You can't want to go outside now. Go back to bed, Morton."

He whined, licked my face and whined again. It became obvious rather quickly that I didn't have another option, so I groaned myself into a sitting position and attempted to wake up. I got to my feet, hurried into the bathroom, and when I came out, I noticed that the table where Barbie had dumped her chips had been cleared off. I peeked into the bedroom to check on her, but there were only feathers scattered around the room. A large pile of makeup, creams, some curlers, hairbrushes, shampoo, and shower gel was mounded in the middle of the bed, but Barbie, and for that matter, Sugar, were nowhere to be seen. I checked the bathroom with the Jacuzzi. It was empty, as were the other two bathrooms.

I attached the leash to Morton's collar and headed for the door. That's when I saw her note. She had folded it and tucked the thing between the door and the brass plate on the doorknob. *'Dev, couldn't sleep and feeling lucky again. Taking Sugar with me. Barbie'.*

I was beginning to think it might have been a good thing Morton woke me up. No telling how long she had been gone. We hurried to the elevator, rode it down to the casino level, and stepped out. The first bit of business was to get Morton doing the task at hand. Once that was accomplished, we could search for the girls. We walked around the block and paused on an empty corner lot long enough for Morton to complete his task. The temperature was already approaching the stifling point.

I was holding the leash, intentionally looking the other way so Morton would have some privacy, when a voice said, "What a well-trained dog. Would you happen to have some spare change? I'm trying to get back to Indiana for my sister's funeral."

I turned and faced an older guy in a Hawaiian print shirt, camouflage shorts, and flip flops. "Excuse me?"

"I said I'm trying to get to Indiana for my sister's funeral, and I wonder if you might have some change you could spare."

"No, sorry, I don't have any. Good luck."

"Luck has nothing to do with it. I'm relying on the generosity of strangers to aid me in my quest, and you, sir, are apparently one hell of a despicable bastard."

I thought about that for half a moment, then nodded and said, "You're probably right. Have a nice trip, where did you say you were going, Illinois?"

"Exactly, no thanks to you."

"I'd love to help you out, but my girlfriend is inside gambling all our money away. I'd better get back inside and try and stop her."

"I can only hope you'll be too late, sir. Good day," he said and strode off down the street. Morton and I hurried back inside to the temperature-controlled climate of the Bellagio and started searching for Barbie.

The first line of craps tables we came to, the same ones Barbie had won so big at the night before, were all closed. I was suddenly attracted by a round of cheers. At the far end of the casino, a crowd had gathered around a table, so we hurried off in that direction. Morton seemed to be picking up speed the closer we got to the crowd. By the time we arrived, he was straining at his leash, and my right arm felt like he was going to pull it out of the socket. I kept saying, "Morton, heel Morton. Morton, sit," repeating myself over and over again. He ignored each and every one of my commands. More cheers and another round of applause rose up from the crowd just as we approached.

I heard the stickman say, "The lady wins on two. Place your bets, place your bets."

Morton suddenly barked, and a number of people looked at him, a few stepped aside and gave us room to pass. A small, high-pitched bark replied to Morton's bark, which could only mean Barbie and Sugar were somewhere in the crowd. At the sound of another high-pitched bark, I looked off to the left and spotted her, Sugar. Barbie had her tucked under her left arm. Barbie was shaking her right hand, and it suddenly dawned on me that it could quite possibly hold a pair of dice.

Morton barked just as Barbie tossed the dice. Sugar barked twice and squirmed to get out from Barbie's grasp, and the crowd cheered.

Barbie turned in our direction, then smiled and nodded as we approached. The crowd cleared a path for us. Morton was straining on the leash, and Sugar was squirming as Barbie attempted to hold her tightly against her chest.

"I felt lucky again," Barbie half-shouted. "And guess what? We're winning."

"I wish you would have woken me, I was worried about you," I said. I didn't bother to explain, I was actually worried about her gambling away all the money she'd won the night before.

"I gave you a kiss, but you were snoring, and I didn't want to wake you. So we just came down here and, well, we're winning."

"Place your bets, place your bets," the stickman said.

Barbie suddenly thrust Sugar at me, then pulled that huge black makeup bag of hers off her shoulder and began shoveling stacks of chips into it. The chips were all different colors, white, green, red, black, and purple. Some of the chips fell on the floor, and two young guys about twenty bent over and began to pick them up. They stood at about the same time, and each dumped a handful of chips into the makeup bag.

Barbie smiled, reached in the bag, pulled out two green chips, and handed one to each of them. Twenty-five bucks each.

Morton was busy licking Sugar. Sugar kept turning her head, apparently, so Morton wouldn't miss a spot.

Barbie stepped toward me and said, "You can buy me breakfast." She linked arms with me, and we walked away from the table as the crowd cheered and clapped.

"Let's go back up to the room and order room service," I said.

Fifteen

It was after three when the phone rang and woke me.

"Hello," I groaned.

"What are you doing in your room?" Goose asked.

I went on to give him a brief explanation of the day's activities, starting with Barbie sneaking back down to gamble and winning again.

"You gotta be kidding me. Maybe we should start doubling up on her bets. She seems to be on a real, honest to God winning streak. Any sign of those guys?"

"The three who were following us? No. I'm beginning to think they may have just been tourists and were hanging around to watch Barbie jump up and down."

"Yeah, except they were the same three that were trying to cozy up to my brother, Kenny."

"Oh, yeah, sorry, I guess I was focused on Barbie winning all that dough. Anyway, I didn't see them this morning."

"Where are you now?"

"I was asleep until you called, hang on a minute. Let me just check and make sure Barbie is still here." I walked over to the bedroom door and quietly pushed it open. Barbie was face down in the bed, sound asleep with her head beneath a pillow. Two Barbie dolls rested on top of the other pillow. Morton was stretched out on the bed, sleeping next to her. Sugar was curled up on the other pillow at the foot of the bed and raised her head, gave me the once over, but apparently couldn't be bothered. She put her head back down on the pillow and closed her eyes. Feathers from the two pillows Morton had destroyed were still scattered across the bedroom floor.

I quietly pulled the bedroom door closed. "She's sound asleep. I guess all that winning can be exhausting."

"I wouldn't know," Goose said. "Hey, I'm knocking off at five this afternoon. I'd like to have you come with me over to The Palms. I've got to pick Kenny up and give him a ride home. You can meet him, check the place out. Bring Barbie. She'll really dig the place."

"Let me see what she says once she wakes up."

"Trust me. She'll like it. They got this Barbie suite and—"

"What?"

"Yeah, a suite of rooms all decorated with Barbie stuff, you know, Barbie the doll."

"You're kidding."

"No, honest to God. It's got framed pictures of Barbie on the walls, a bunch of dolls all over the place, life-size stuff from her dollhouse. It's crazy."

"She'd love to see it."

"Let me call Kenny, if the room is open, he'll have someone arrange a tour for you guys. I'll touch base with you in about an hour and a half."

"Thanks, Goose. Talk to you later." I turned off my cell, then checked the cabinets in the kitchen area. They were all empty. I picked up the phone, called room service, and ordered a corned beef on rye and a Coke. It arrived forty-five minutes later. I ate the sandwich while looking out the window at the traffic below. The temperature outside was a hundred and seven. The four-lane strip below was jammed with cars and trucks, mobs of people filled the sidewalks and pedestrian overpasses.

I heard Barbie in the bathroom just as my cell rang.

"Yeah, Goose."

"You want to head over to The Palms in about an hour?"

"Yeah, I haven't talked to Barbie yet, she's just waking up, but I'm sure she'll want to see the doll stuff. How 'bout we meet you down in the lobby at five?"

"Sounds good. Kenny's lining someone up to show us the Barbie suite. I have to punch out and change, so make it closer to a quarter after."

"See you then," I said just as Barbie stepped out of the bedroom, tracking a little trail of feathers along with her.

"Oh, wow, I must have needed that. I was dead to the world. Did you get any sleep?" She had pulled on her pink silk dressing gown, which was failing miserably at covering her up. She wore a pink silk thong sporting a

Barbie signature across the front in a darker pink. I just stood and stared. "Dev?"

"Huh? Oh, hey, I just got off the phone with Goose. We're going to meet him down in the lobby in a little over an hour. He's going to take us to The Palms, that's where his brother works. I thought you might like to check it out."

"Oh, you go ahead, I think I might just go down to the casino here and wander around."

"You mean you're going to go down there and play craps again."

"I'm feeling lucky again, Dev. What can I tell you?"

"I think you might like The Palms."

"Thanks, but you go ahead, make it a guys night. Don't worry. I'll be just fine here."

"Honey, you're up over fifty grand, that can do a lot for you. Think about cashing out a winner and bringing that money home. Hey, you could paint the entire interior of your place pink, get an all new wardrobe, and have money left over to buy a new pink convertible." I was joking, but I could see the wheels turning.

Eventually, she shook her head. "No, I'm feeling lucky, so I think it might be better if I just stayed here."

"Okay, suit yourself. I'll let you know what the suites look like at The Palms."

"The suites?"

"Yeah, Goose's brother works there as an accountant or something. Apparently, they have a number of different theme suites, erotic, celebrity. I guess they've even have a Barbie suite."

"What?" she shouted. "A Barbie suite?"

"Yeah, Goose's brother is setting up a tour, so I'll let you know what it was like. I don't know, maybe I'll get some ideas for your place, I mean if I can remember all the stuff. Hey, where are you going?"

"Well, I can't very well go like this. You know, while I'm getting ready, you could take Sugar and Morton down to the dog spa."

"The dog spa?"

"Yes, please, and thank you. They get some playtime, a massage, a bath. They'll love it."

"What's that cost?"

"Dev, I'm feeling lucky, remember. Maybe just take them down there, they can get groomed while we're at The Palms. Ooooooh, a Barbie suite, I can't wait," she squealed then hurried back into the bathroom.

Sixteen

I attached the respective leashes to both dogs, then took the elevator down to the main floor. There was a security guy in a red blazer with a white earphone attached to his ear.

"Hi, I wanted to take these two to the dog spa. Apparently, you have such a place here."

He smiled and nodded. "Yeah, we call it the Groom Room, hop back on the elevator, go down one more level, you'll see signs for it as soon as you step off the elevator."

"Thanks," I said.

Just as I turned to get back on the elevator, I caught something out of the corner of my eye. It was one of the three guys I'd seen last night. One of the three Goose was worried about. His back was to me now, and he was pretending to look in a store window across the way. The shop featured purses and handbags. Maybe he had a girlfriend he was shopping for. Maybe he thought he'd look good with one. I didn't know, and so I ignored the impulse to walk over and tap him on the shoulder. Instead, I got back onto the elevator and went down to the next level.

A sign indicating the Groom Room was the first thing that greeted me when I stepped off the elevator. The arrow on the sign pointed to the right. A trail of paw prints was embedded in the floor tiles and led us right to the door. I stepped into a fancy sort of waiting room with a girl maybe eighteen or nineteen sitting behind a receptionist counter.

"Welcome," she said before I'd even closed the door behind me. "Who do we have here?" she asked, coming around the counter. She wore a gold name tag that said Ramona, and she reached down and scratched Morton behind the ear, which sent his tail slapping against my leg.

"That's Morton."

Sugar barked, and the girl said, "I was just getting to you, darling." Then she picked Sugar up. "Oh, aren't you cute, and so tiny."

"That's Sugar."

"Sugar. Like Barbie's dog?"

"One and the same, that's who she's named after." I saw no point in saying anything beyond that.

"Did you have an appointment?"

"An appointment? No, we didn't. I was hoping for a massage for both of them, plus a bath and grooming."

"Are you on any particular time frame?"

"Time frame?"

"The massage, bath, and grooming will take about two and a half hours. With two of them, you may want to leave them for at least three hours, maybe longer. We close at nine, so that's cutting it kind of close. If you don't make it back before nine, we'll board them overnight."

"That sounds perfect. Not sure when I'll be able to get back," I said, thinking I could actually have the bed with Barbie in it all to myself tonight. And if I wasn't back down here until, oh, say, maybe ten tomorrow morning, someone else would have to deal with the morning duties. Perfect.

She took down our room number, Morton's and Sugar's names. Asked a series of questions about allergies, food preferences, and bedtimes, then said, "Very good, Mr. Haskell, we'll look forward to seeing you tomorrow."

I took the elevator back up to the main floor, stepped out, and looked around for the guy I'd seen earlier but couldn't find him. I got back on the elevator and rode up to our room.

"Is that you, Dev?" Barbie called from the bedroom.

"Yeah, it's just me. I dropped thing one and thing two off in the Groom Room, they close at nine, and they'll keep them overnight if we don't make it back in time," I said, walking into the bedroom. I noticed a sleek pink dress laid out on the bed. A matching pair of pink high heels with gold toe caps were sitting on the floor in front of the bed, Barbie's signature in black was scrolled across the toe of the shoe just above the toe cap.

I leaned against the bathroom door while Barbie remained focused on the makeup mirror. She was carefully working with a brush. "Did Sugar seem happy?" she asked, not looking at me.

"Yeah, real nice girl down there, Ramona."

"It's her time."

"What?"

"Sugar. Wouldn't you know, she's in heat just when we take a vacation. It never ends."

"Ramona was holding Sugar when I left and giving her a kiss. They'll both be fine." For the first time, I noticed the pink bracelet on her left wrist. It was edged in gold with the word 'FABULOUS' in a darker pink, along with a silhouette of what I guessed was Barbie wearing a ponytail. I didn't say anything.

"I'll be ready to go in a few minutes," she said. "What are you going to wear?"

"These jeans and I've got a St. Paul Saints t-shirt that's kind of clean in my suitcase, I think."

She flashed a smile meant to be anything but pleasant. "No. I checked online, this suite at The Palms looks really wonderful, and I want you looking your best. There's a shirt to wear hanging in the closet behind you."

"You're kidding." I stepped over to the closet and opened the louvered french doors. There was a shelf with two more pillows and an iron. An ironing board was folded and hanging on the back wall. There was just a single item hanging in the closet, a pink and white pin-striped shirt. The collar was solid pink and looked starched, the buttons were pink, and on the sleeve where a monogram would be was a darker pink silhouette of

Barbie with a ponytail. Just like the one on the bracelet my Barbie was wearing.

"A Barbie shirt? Are you kidding? No 'f'ing way."

"Oh, really?" she said calmly, then stood and brushed her cleavage with the makeup brush. She proceeded to make a show of admiring her handiwork in the large mirror above the vanity before she turned to face me. She was wearing a pink silk thong and a smile. The thong had the same dark pink silhouette of Barbie that was on the shirt and the bracelet. She squirted some hand cream into her hand, smiled, and began rubbing her hands together. "Would you like to reconsider that last comment?" she asked and raised her eyebrows.

"Let me see if that shirt fits."

"Smart man," she said, then kissed me on the cheek as she walked past into the bedroom. "If you hurry, you'll have just enough time to take a quick shower."

I shaved in the shower, washed quickly, then dried off. I tried on my Barbie shirt, and unfortunately, it fit. I tried to convince myself that maybe I was just overreacting, but then I looked at the monogrammed silhouette of Barbie's head on the shirt sleeve and knew I wasn't. It was liable to be open season on me tonight.

"Can you zip me up?" she called from the bedroom.

I walked back into the bedroom as she was looking at herself in the full-length mirror. The pink dress had darker beaded spaghetti straps and beads along the edge of the plunging neckline. She turned away from me as I walked in so I could zip her up, the back of the dress was open halfway down her back. I didn't notice any tan lines.

"I'm thinking we should just stay in tonight, Barbie, you look absolutely beautiful."

"You mean fabulous," she laughed, then shook her wrist with the bracelet. "Come on, let's go meet Goose."

Seventeen

It started with the security guard at the elevators on the ground floor. He raised his eyebrows as Barbie passed by, nodded, and said, "Nice, very nice." It was a version of Moses parting the waters as we walked through the casino toward the hotel lobby. Men and women stepped aside and stared as she walked past, I stumbled along in her wake. I felt like I was Barbie's servant as people stared and pointed. A few of them whispered, a couple of folks shook their heads. I guessed they were trying to figure out what movie star they were looking at. Either that or they were wondering who the flunky was in the pink pinstriped shirt with the Barbie monogram following behind her.

We stood in a corner of the lobby for a few minutes before Goose showed up. I saw him hustling across the lobby, then slowing his approach as he drew closer. "Wow, Barbie, you look fantastic. Come on," he said, holding his arm out to her. "Let me escort you."

"Thanks, Goose." She smiled, shrugged, then linked arms with him.

Goose focused on her bounce for just a moment before the two of them headed for the revolving doors leading outside. "Oh, hi, Dev," he mumbled over his shoulder just as they stepped into one of the sections of the automatically revolving door. I had to wait until the next section came around, then watched the two of them laughing together ahead of me.

"The three of us are going to The Palms," Goose said to the guy directing the line of folks getting into taxi cabs, then he turned to me. "Hey, Dev, you got a buck or two you can slip him?"

The guy jumped forward and opened the door once the taxi stopped. He made an overly gracious bow as Barbie strutted past and climbed into the back seat. The three of us stared at her for a long moment, enjoying the view. Goose hurried around to the far side of the cab and called over the roof, "You can just get in the front seat, Dev." He pulled the rear door open, slid in next to Barbie, slammed the door closed and locked it as I came around the back of the cab.

I gave him a quick glance suggesting I wasn't too happy, then opened the front passenger door and climbed in. The taxi driver glanced at me, then checked his rearview mirror and adjusted it so he could see Barbie. "The Palms, you said?"

"Yeah," Goose replied before he half-turned in the back seat and focused in on Barbie. "You're going to love the tour. I got my younger brother to line it up just for you. The suite has a Barbie theme, and no one is there tonight, so we can take just as long as you want. I've made special arrangements so you can—"

"Is your brother going to be with us?" I asked.

"Yeah, I told him to be there," he said, then refocused on Barbie. "I've made some special arrangements so you'll get the deluxe tour. They have hand-stitched pillows on the bed, just like in the Barbie playhouse."

"Really! The Playhouse or the deluxe model?" She was serious.

"Oh, ahhh, I'm not sure which one, but I know the person giving us the tour will be able to answer that. Now, there's a special Barbie curtain that you brush aside to go into the—"

"You're sure your brother is going to be there?"

"Yeah, I—"

"Dev, Goose is trying to tell me about the Barbie suite, and you're ruining it. I don't want to hear another word from you until after we're finished with the tour."

"After we're finished with the—"

"I mean it, Dev. Now, be quiet."

Neither Goose nor I said anything. The only sound in the taxi was the cab driver softly humming '*Kiss Me Once and Kiss Me Twice.*' Mercifully, we made it through the next two green lights, and the driver went from humming to talking. "That's it just up there," he said as we emerged from beneath a freeway overpass.

There were three tall glass buildings glowing against the sky. One had a sort of rounded top with the name 'PALMS' emblazoned in white across the top and along the side of the structure. The building next to it featured what looked like a Playboy bunny halfway up the side.

"Wow," Barbie said.

"Pretty cool, isn't it?" Goose said.

"That'll be twenty-two fifty," the cab driver said as he pulled to the curb. Goose hustled out of the cab, then walked around the side and held the door open for Barbie, which left me to pay the tab. "Twenty-two fifty," the driver said again and smiled.

I handed him a twenty and a ten and said, "Just give me a couple of one's back."

He peeled two dollar bills from a thick stack of cash, handed me two bucks, and said, "Enjoy your evening."

I nodded, climbed out of the taxi, and the heat hit me like a bus. As our taxi pulled away, another one pulled in right behind it. I had to hurry to catch up to Goose and Barbie, who were already halfway to the entrance of The Palms. I didn't reach them until they were entering the building. Goose had his phone out and up against his ear. He pointed it toward the sky as he talked to me.

"I'm just calling my brother to let him know we're here. I want to see if he can . . . Hey, man, we're down here in the lobby, Kenny. You got time to show us around? Oh. No, I suppose that will work. Yeah. Just inside the main entrance. Okay, what does she look like? Okay. Okay. Yeah, it's me and Dev Haskell, no he's wearing a girlie blouse," Goose laughed. "We're with a very beautiful woman with blonde hair and a gorgeous pink outfit that everybody in here is staring at. Yeah, okay. We'll keep an eye out for her."

Goose disconnected and looked around for a brief moment, pretending to scan the lobby. I knew him well enough to know he'd just been thrown a curve. "I guess he's just a little busy right now, my brother. He's sending someone down who'll take us up to the Barbie suite for a tour. She thinks we're looking to rent the place, so, you know, sort of play along."

Barbie smiled and moved her hands up and down excitedly. "Oh, God, I can't wait. I'm going to take a ton of pictures," she said.

"They should be down here in five or ten minutes."

Barbie seemed oblivious to the crowd of people staring at her. Heads turned, people walking past slowed down. Just standing there, she was creating somewhat of a pedestrian traffic jam in the lobby. Two little boys about ten approached her with an envelope in hand and asked her for her autograph. She didn't even blink, pulled a pink sharpie from her purse, and gave them her one-word autograph, Barbie. She asked them where they were from; Manhattan, Kansas, by the way. They chatted for a good minute or two before the kids skipped away, happy and waving the autograph.

It was another thirty minutes before our tour guide arrived. Actually, there were three of them, two women and a guy. "Mr. Gander?" one of the women asked.

Goose smiled, looked more than a little relieved they had finally shown up, and said, "That's me."

"So sorry for the delay," she turned and faced Barbie. "Janice Hart, by the way," she said and held her hand out.

"Barbie."

The three of them looked at one another and smiled, but not in a way that suggested they were laughing at her. More like they'd just won a big prize. "So very nice to meet you. This is Camille, and Tom Diamond, who heads up our marketing department. I, or, rather, we were watching you on the security cameras."

Barbie gave a little frown.

"Oh, nothing bad, I assure you. It's just that your resemblance to the actual Barbie doll…"

"And that's really my name, Barbie Dahl."

"That's spelled D-A-H-L," I inserted.

Barbie glared at me.

Tom Diamond rubbed his hands together and said, "We would love to show you the suite. Let's take the private elevator, and we can talk on the way, Miss Dahl. May I call you Barbie?"

"Everyone does," Barbie giggled.

Diamond turned to lead the way, scanned the people watching us, and half-whispered to his accomplices, "You two were right, just look at this crowd."

As we headed out, I thought I caught a glimpse of the same guy I'd seen back at the Bellagio, one of the three guys Goose was worried about. He was hanging back on the edge of the crowd. I remembered the cab pulling in right behind us when we first arrived and wondered if he had been in it. Just as quickly, he seemed to disappear, and I had to hurry to catch up to Barbie and her new entourage.

Eighteen

The private elevator was just that, private and elegant. The Palms folks were polite and clearly focused on Barbie. Goose and I were apparently just along for the ride. Tom Diamond continued to bombard Barbie with compliments.

"I hope you won't be offended, but you bear a striking resemblance to the Barbie doll. And your surname is spelled, D-A-H-L? You didn't have it changed?"

"No, it's on my birth certificate. All the girls in primary school were jealous of my name."

"And high school?" Janice asked.

"Jealous for other reasons," Barbie said with a cold smile.

"I think you're going to love the suite," Diamond said. "We're in the midst of planning an entirely new marketing campaign. We've discovered that Barbie seems to be a universal experience for all American girls. I'd love to get your thoughts."

"Well, my first thought would be that Barbie is an experience for girls all over the world." The elevator stopped on the twenty-sixth floor, the bell rang, and the doors opened. Diamond indicated Barbie should step off first, and then he quickly stepped alongside her, cutting the rest of us off as she continued.

"Three Barbies are sold somewhere in the world every second of every day. She's banned in Saudi Arabia. I forget the exact number, but she's had something like a hundred and twenty-five careers. Did you know that she's served in every branch of the armed forces? She—"

Goose and I drifted back a few paces. What was the big deal? It was just a doll, after all. Goose looked at me and rolled his eyes. Barbie was in the process of answering a question Diamond asked.

"That would be Betina Dorfman. I believe she still has the largest Barbie collection in the world. Amazingly, it's in Germany. She also established a Barbie clinic."

"A clinic, do they do implants?" Janice half-laughed.

"Hardly," Barbie said and glared. "No, they repair Barbies, restore them to their original beauty."

"I think I can take it from here, Janice," Diamond said, effectively dismissing her. She nodded, turned, then flared her eyes and seemed to be biting her lip as she barreled past Goose and I and back down the hall.

"You were saying, Miss Dahl."

"Please, I prefer Barbie."

"Certainly," he said, then pulled a magnetic key from his suit coat pocket and opened the door to the Barbie suite. The entry was circular, with Barbie wallpaper on the walls. Barbie stood there in the hallway, quiet, at least for a brief moment, and took it all in.

Diamond stepped through the entry and into a nightmare of pink and sparkles. "This was designed by a man named Jonathan Adler, he—"

"The same man who did the Real-Life Malibu Dream House?"

"Why, yes, he did. I have to say you, ahh, sure know your Barbie. Champagne?" he asked, then took a crystal flute from a bowl of ice resting on the bar, poured champagne into it, and handed it to Barbie.

"Oh, look, that's classic Barbie and Malibu Barbie," Barbie said, then raised her flute in a toast to two large paintings on the wall.

"Strawberry?" Diamond asked and held a silver dish out to her with strawberries. The two of them wandered into the living room area, more garish pink with a pink and white tiled floor with pink sparkles. They seemed to be topping one another with bits of Barbie trivia as they wandered through the suite, oblivious to Goose, Camille, and myself.

"They got any beer?" Goose asked, looking at the silver bucket holding the bottle of champagne.

"Just the champagne, I'm afraid," Camille said.

"Can I pour you some?" I asked and began filling a flute.

"Oh, I better not," she said, and for the first time, I noticed the manila file folder she carried in her right hand.

"God, I'm getting a headache from this place, and we've only been in here for a minute or two. I don't think pink is my color," I said.

"You'd be surprised how popular this suite is. It's routinely booked out for at least a year in advance. We're lucky it's even available."

"You're kidding."

"No, it's quite popular. A lot of bachelorette parties, the occasional honeymoon couple, and a lot of couples who just think it would be fun."

"I don't get it."

Barbie and Diamond were in the process of wandering into the master bedroom suite. You could almost hear the various shades of pink screaming from the walls.

"There's, ahhh, something for everyone. Here, let me show you," Camille said, then turned in the opposite direction to lead us into the master bathroom. There was a large marble-topped vanity, a full-length mirror, and chairs where I guess your guests could watch you take a bath.

"This is the shower room. It has these jets that spray you from the side, then the rain shower from the ceiling and, of course, this chrome stripper pole which could lead to all sorts of possible ways to, ahh, exercise in the shower."

"That's got my vote," Goose said.

"I have to agree."

"Yes, quite popular with our male guests, Barbie's been known to be fun for everyone."

"Oh, you beat us to it," Diamond said, then stepped into the shower room with Barbie. "Note the chrome dance pole and . . ." he said, flicking a switch. Suddenly, pink, green, and blue lights flashed off and on, illuminating the shower like a stripper's stage.

Barbie laughed, then took hold of the pole and spun around three or four times like a pro.

Diamond grinned and quietly clapped his hands together until she stopped spinning. "Wonderful, wonderful. Note the foil wallpaper. The design is actually made up of lower case 'b's. B for Barbie," he smiled.

"It's absolutely gorgeous," Barbie said.

Goose and I shot a glance at one another.

"So you like it?" Diamond said.

"Like it? No, I love it. It's, it's like my dream come true."

"Would you like to stay here for the night?"

"You mean it's available?" She fluttered her hands, suggesting she couldn't believe her luck. I wondered if the place came with aspirin and a sleeping mask.

"Well, it's not officially available, but if you'd care to be our guest and, ahh, of course, Mr. Gander," Diamond said, looking questioningly at Goose.

"Actually, I'm with the other one, Dev," Barbie said, sounding sort of disappointed as she nodded at me.

"Of course," Diamond said, all smiles. "Let's all take a seat in the living room. I've got a proposition I think you're going to like. You've got the file with the contracts, Camille?"

"Yes, sir."

Diamond, Camille, and Goose headed out to the living room. Barbie grabbed my arm and whispered, "Ooooh, Dev, I don't believe it. Isn't this exciting?"

Nineteen

Diamond sat down on the black leather couch, wedged between two pink pillows emblazoned with the letter 'B.' "Barbie, please, dear, come join me on the couch," he said and patted the cushion next to him.

Goose and I sat down in two upholstered chairs with a fabric pattern of Barbie images. Both chairs had a large pink shoelace crisscrossing up the back like a giant corset. Camille walked over, handed Barbie a flute of champagne, then gave one to Diamond. She was back a moment later with champagne flutes for Goose and me.

The champagne was wasted on me, it could have been five hundred bucks a bottle, and it wouldn't have mattered. I'd never know the difference, and, to tell the truth, I would have been happier with a cold beer.

"How about a toast to, well, to Barbie, the doll, and to you, Barbie Dahl," Diamond said and raised his champagne flute.

Barbie was so excited that she could only nod and smile. Goose and I were forced to take a sip with the toast.

"Now, here's what I'm thinking," Diamond said. "Why don't you stay here for the night? Be our guest in the Barbie suite. I gotta tell you, Barbie, from the moment I saw you on our security cameras, I knew you were a natural. I knew you were the one I wanted. The one we had to have for our campaign."

Barbie took a large swallow of champagne and coughed, not looking too sure about what she'd just heard.

"What Mr. Diamond is trying to say, Barbie," Camille said, hurrying across the room and placing the manila file folder on the coffee table in front of Barbie, "Is that we are in the process of interviewing models for a photoshoot to update our advertising for all our suites. We've been looking at portfolios for weeks and weeks and still haven't found the right person to photograph for the Barbie suite. That is until we saw you on the cameras today."

"You'd be perfect, Barbie," Diamond said. "You're just the person we've been looking for. Of course, you'd stay here as our guest. In fact, you could stay here for the entire photoshoot. Make a note, Camille, cancel whoever made reservations until we're finished shooting. Oh, and how does this sound, our Barbie wardrobe, it's yours, all yours. We take your picture in it, and the outfit, any outfit, is yours to keep."

"Ohhhh," Barbie squealed and sort of shook all over, even Camille seemed to pay attention to her figure at that point.

"Now, the photoshoot could begin the day after to-morrow," Diamond went on. "How long were you planning to be out here?"

"Actually," I said, ready to rain on this particular parade. "We're heading home in just a day or two, so I don't think . . ."

Diamond turned to face Barbie, which put his back to me. He gave a half-shrug as if to say 'that was no big deal.' "I know, we'll simply book you a flight home, Barbie, how does that sound? First-class, of course, and, like I said, you can simply stay here in the Barbie suite until the photoshoot is finished. We've allowed a couple of days for the shoot, but that was before we saw you. I think now we'd like to have a minimum of four days for the shoot, union rate remuneration, of course," he nodded.

"Dev?"

"Well, the tickets we got are nonrefundable. So, sorry, but I don't think…"

"Not a problem, you can head home, Hassle, get back to whatever it is you do, and Barbie, you can follow up just as soon as we're finished. I tell you what, Camille, clear it with the folks downstairs and let's set Barbie up with a thousand-dollar nest egg she can gamble away in the casino. All the folks stopping to stare, we'd love to have you playing at our tables. Might just turn that into a photoshoot, too, now that I think of it. How does that sound?"

"Like I said, those airline tickets are nonrefundable, so I don't think it would be . . . ."

"Yes, yes," Barbie squealed, then rocked back and forth on the couch. Diamond and Goose gave an appreciative stare. "Dev, you can just head home without me. I'll catch up when I've finished this photoshoot. Ooooh, a Barbie photoshoot. Mr. Diamond, this is a dream come true for me."

"Wonderful, Camille, do you have a pen ready? Let's have Barbie sign those contracts before someone steals her away from us," Diamond said, then worked his damnedest not to look at me.

There was a knock on the door at that point. Camille stared at everyone as if to ask, 'Who could that be?' before she went to answer the door.

"Oh, hi, thanks for coming," we heard her say. A moment later, she walked back into the room with a young guy. He was blonde, tan, and looked familiar, although it took me a moment before I caught on. Goose's younger brother, Kenny. He was probably just twelve or thirteen the last time I had seen him.

"Hey, Kenny," Goose smiled and rose out of his Barbie chair.

I got to my feet and held out my hand. "Long time no see, Kenny. You're looking good."

He shook my hand but didn't look directly at me, he never did. "Nice to see you, Dev. How do you like Las Vegas?"

"It's changed a lot since the last time I was here, it's . . . interesting."

"Camille, get Ken a glass of champagne, will you?" Diamond said.

"Kenny, this is a friend of mine, Barbie Dahl, she came out here with me."

"Oh, umm, hi," he mumbled, then waved at her and looked at his feet for a long moment.

"It's nice to meet you, Ken," she said and then erased her smile a moment later and shot a vicious glance at me.

"Oh, wow, your name is Barbie, and you're in the Barbie suite, and you even really look like her, too," Kenny said.

"See, there you go," Diamond said. "Camille, hand me that pen. Now, Barbie, if you would sign here, please, where the line is highlighted in yellow."

"You might want to read through that to make sure…"

"I'm sure it's just fine," Barbie said and glared at me, then switched to a sexy smile as she signed on the dotted line.

"Yes, wonderful. Humf, and that's really your legal signature? It looks exactly like Barbie's," Diamond said.

"I know, I've practiced it since I was a little girl, now it's, well, it's just natural."

"Amazing, this just keeps getting better and better all the time," he said, flipping a page on the contract. "Now, if you'll just initial these three areas, then one more page to sign." He flipped to the final page once she'd written her initials. "Perfect, and sign there, and then if you'd write in your social security number, we'll be ready to go. Camille, if you would coordinate with the front desk and have room keys up here for Miss, excuse me, for Barbie. Oh, and have that thousand-dollar credit lined up. Folks, it's been a real pleasure," Diamond said, getting to his feet.

"I've enjoyed meeting you, Mr. Hassle, and you, too," he said to Goose, obviously having forgotten anything close to Goose's name. "I look forward to working with you, Barbie. I'd better hurry back and begin to get things set up. I want to see if we can start shooting tomorrow. We're going to have a wonderful time, absolutely wonderful. Thank you, come along, Camille, we'll let these people celebrate," he said and headed for the door.

I waited until the door closed, then looked at Barbie. "Honey, you signed those contracts? What are you thinking? Did you even read the damn things?"

"Dev, I'm the star in a Barbie photoshoot. What's to think about?"

"Well, for starters, we had flight reservations and—"

"And they're flying me home, first-class, I might add, once I finish these photoshoots."

"Well, you booked that room for us at the Bellagio, the place where you were so lucky at the tables."

"Oh, I'd say my luck has been running pretty good here. By the way, I could do with a little more champagne," she said and held up her empty champagne flute. I couldn't believe it and just stared at her.

"Here you go," Kenny said and emptied the bottle into her glass.

"Why, thank you, Ken. Mind if I ask when your birthday is?"

"My birthday? March eleventh, why?"

"Incredible," Barbie said. "Dev, why don't you open that other bottle and get Ken a glass of champagne? Here, Ken, come sit next to me. You can tell me all about the places I should see while I'm out here in Las Vegas. Dev, are you getting that champagne?"

"I'm on it," I said, sounding none too happy about it. I opened the other bottle, poured the champagne into a flute, then walked over to the couch and handed it to Kenny.

"Thank you," Barbie smiled, meaning anything but 'thank you.' "I wonder if it wouldn't be a good idea if you hurried back to the Bellagio and got the luggage?"

"The Bellagio? Barbie, you reserved that suite for the two of us for all four nights. I thought that's where you wanted to stay."

"Then you can just bring my luggage," she said and flashed a rather cold smile. "Dev, can I talk to you for a moment, please?" She stood, ran her hand through Kenny's hair, and said to him, "Wait here, this should only take a moment. Dev, if you'd follow me, please."

I followed her into the master bathroom. She turned to face me, took a sip of champagne, and leaned against the stripper pole in the shower. "Look, Dev. I don't know if this is working. Maybe a night apart would give us some time to calm down and let both of us think things through."

"Calm down?"

"Stop it, please, you're shouting."

"No, I'm not," I shouted.

"Dev, I feel we need some space, some time apart. Now, are you going to get my luggage, or do you want me to take a taxi all the way back to the Bellagio?"

"Time apart? I, I flew us out here. You booked that suite for four nights. I babysat you while you gambled. I got the tour of this stupid, life-sized dollhouse, arranged for you and now we need some time apart?"

"Yes. Exactly."

"What did I do?"

"If I have to spell it out for you then, well okay. I'll just take a taxi back to get my luggage, and then I'll take a taxi back over here to…"

"I'll get your damn luggage, Barbie, it's just that…"

"We both need a little time, Dev. That temper of yours…"

"My temper, what the hell…"

"You're shouting again."

"Can't I get my luggage, too, and we could, you know, maybe try out this shower room, just to see…"

"There you go, that's what it always comes down to, isn't it?"

I was wondering, *'What else is there?'* but decided it might be wise to keep that particular thought to myself. "Okay, okay. I'll go back to the Bellagio. I'll get your damn luggage, and then I'll bring it back here."

"Thank you, and don't forget Sugar."

Twenty

Goose was attempting to calm me. "I don't know if you can really blame her, Dev. It sounds like she got a hell of a deal, and, well, no offense, but she does seem just a little obsessed with the whole Barbie thing if you don't mind my saying."

"I think she just dumped me in that Barbie shower room."

"Maybe give her some time and space. She'll spend the night in that Barbie suite, wake up in the morning and realize she screwed up. Besides, do you really want to spend a night in that place?"

"I was thinking of some things we could have done that might be fun."

We were about fifth in line outside The Palms, waiting for a taxi so I could get Barbie's luggage. We'd been standing out here for all of about two minutes, and I had already sweated through my Barbie shirt. It was after six, and the temp had dropped to a sweltering hundred and nine Fahrenheit. A guy in a top hat and a black coat was up ahead busily shoving a couple into the next taxi. Thank God I wasn't wearing his outfit.

"Maybe she just needs a break. You know how they get. Just give her some space, maybe let her take the night off," Goose said.

"And then she goes ape-shit because of your brother's birthday on March eleventh."

"Yeah, that was weird. I mean, she looked at his driver's license to make sure he wasn't lying, what the hell was that about? She must have some hot button about St. Patrick's day, too. No offense, but you can sure pick 'em."

"St. Patrick's day? That's the seventeenth, you idiot, no, March eleventh is Ken's birthday, Barbie's boy-friend."

"Her boyfriend? You mean she's two-timing some guy with you?"

"God, Goose. Barbie, the real Barbie, that damn doll."

The guy in the top hat asked where we were headed, then gave a look at my Barbie shirt. Patches of sweat had soaked through beneath both arms along with a large patch on my chest, and I think I could feel one across my back, too. He looked at my shirt, caught sight of the Bar-bie logo monogrammed on the cuff, and directed his at-tention toward Goose. "Where to, gents?"

"The Bellagio," Goose said.

The guy pulled open the rear door of the taxi, and I slid in, Goose piled in after me. The guy shouted, "The Bellagio," to the taxi driver, and we took off.

"She'll cool down by tomorrow, you'll see," Goose said. "Let's get her stuff, bring it back to her, and then you and me and Kenny will make a night of it. We can…"

"What the hell?" the driver suddenly shouted as he made a sharp turn and skidded to the curb. A black paneled van suddenly screeched to a stop in front of us. It was angled against the curb, so we couldn't move forward. I looked out the back window, and another vehicle, a red pickup of some kind had pulled in behind us so we couldn't back up. The taxi driver snapped the locks closed on the doors, then glanced frantically from side to side, looking for a way out. "What the hell have you two gotten me into?"

"Oh, shit," Goose said, looking out the back. Then he quickly turned and faced the front just as someone knocked on the side window and motioned us out with a wiggle of his index finger.

"What the hell is this?" I whispered.

"It's those bastards that have been trying to be pals with Kenny," Goose said.

"Just get the hell out of my cab," the driver yelled and unsnapped the locks. "Go on, you two heard me, get your ass out of my damn cab."

Both rear passenger doors opened simultaneously, and a voice said, "Gentlemen, if we could have a moment of your time. Now."

"I ain't got nothing at all to do with these two. They just put 'em in my cab, and I was stuck with 'em. Driving them to the Bellagio just as fast as I can to get rid of them," our driver shouted.

"If you would, please," the guy holding the door on my side said in a tone that suggested no other option. I slid across the seat and stepped out of the taxi. "Thank you, Mr. Haskell," he said, then indicated the black paneled van angled across the front of the taxi. I headed in that direction, wondering if I could outrun him, deciding almost immediately that would be a bad idea.

The side door to the van opened as we approached, and a guy stepped out onto the curb. I recognized him as the same guy I thought I'd seen earlier at the Bellagio and again while we were waiting in the lobby of The Palms before being escorted up to the Barbie suite. He flashed an insincere smile and gave a slight nod, indicating we should climb into the van.

The driver glanced at us but didn't say anything. I noticed he had a deep scar that ran across the tip of his nose.

There weren't any seats in the back of the van, and we crawled onto the floor. There was a large guy with a shaved head sitting in the rear of the van. He wore a black t-shirt with white letters that read, 'Black Olives Matter.' The t-shirt appeared way too small.

He watched us climb in, then said, "We're just here to talk. We don't want any trouble. Okay?" He smiled, exposing a couple of missing teeth, and I wasn't all that sure things were going to be okay. As the van quickly pulled away from the curb, I half-slid closer to shaved head sitting against the rear door. I grabbed onto the side of the van and inched my way back up toward the front again.

"Sorry for all the drama," the guy in the front passenger seat turned around and said. "Federal agents." He wore a gold ring on the ring finger of his right hand. The ring sported what looked like a fairly large diamond. I picked up a strong scent of cigarette smoke as he turned and talked. He quickly flashed a badge toward me and held it there for a brief second before he snapped the black leather case closed. The badge was gold, round, with an eagle sitting on top of it.

"You guys are tough to get hold of. We've been trying to arrange a meeting ever since you came to town."

"A meeting? About what? Couldn't you just have called? We're staying at…"

"The Bellagio, yeah, we know. Thought it might be better if we just kept things, you know, on a more social level."

"Forcing our taxi to the side of a busy street, pinning it to the curb, then hauling us out of the thing is your idea of social?"

He looked at me for a long moment, then nodded to the driver, who put on the blinker. He seemed to collect his thoughts before he spoke, "You work for Tubby Gustafson, right?"

"No, I don't work for Tubby Gus…"

"We know he met with you. You told him to meet you in your office, didn't you?"

Goose shot me a sheepish look.

"No, I didn't tell him to…no one tells Tubby Gustafson what to do, especially someone like me."

"And yet he sent you out here to Las Vegas on an errand, and then, low and behold you link up with your friend here, who just happens to have a brother studying numbers and percentages at The Palms."

Goose's eyes grew wide, "I, I don't know anything about any of this. Whatever he did," Goose nodded at me. "It was all his idea. I'm not involved in any way, shape, or form. I just want to be left alone. And, and my little brother, too," he added for good measure.

"Haskell?"

"What? I came out here because he was worried about some creeps trying to get close to his brother. Turns out, it was you guys all along. And the only reason Tubby Gustafson was in my office was to threaten me. Goose landed back here in Vegas last Tuesday and asked his boss about Tubby," I gave Goose a glare. "Tubby heard about that thirty minutes later, and the next thing I know, he's in my office interrupting my work. I didn't know anything about it. I don't know anything about any connection Tubby has out here. I don't know anything, honest. I really don't know a thing."

"You don't know a thing? That's probably the most honest line you've uttered all day. Okay, Danny, pull over. Gentlemen, we're going to let you out. We'll just let this serve as a warning, don't go sticking your nose where it don't belong. Oh, and nice Barbie shirt," he said, then laughed. "Go on, get the hell out of here before we change our minds." He reached over the seat and opened the side door a few inches, then nodded at me to slide it all the way back.

As we stepped out of the van, the heat seemed to smother us. It was heading toward dusk, and we were standing in the middle of nowhere, in the midst of what looked like miles of red dirt and construction rubble. Nothing but rocks and dried, thorny weeds for as far as we could see.

"Enjoy the walk home," someone called from inside the van. They all laughed and then floored the van, which sent a hail of rocks flying in our direction and a cloud of dust floating down that settled over the two of us. Once the dust settled, we could see the lights from the Las Vegas skyline off in the distance.

"You gotta be shitting me," Goose said. "Those bastards just left us out here?"

"I'm just glad they're gone. How far is it to town?"

"You don't want to know."

"Then we better get started. Come on, Goose, let's get going."

* * *

We'd been walking for hours, and my feet were killing me. We were both sunburned and thirsty as hell. At least we were on pavement now, not that anyone bothered to stop and pick us up when we stuck out our thumbs. Another car shot past us, some woman behind the wheel wearing hundred dollar sunglasses and a designer top who couldn't be bothered to even look, let alone stop. She probably had the air conditioning turned up on high.

"I still don't get it. Why do three FBI agents want to become pals with Kenny? Why don't they just talk to him over coffee? He'd think it was really cool, figure he was in a movie or on TV or something," Goose said.

"You get a look at that badge of his?"

"Not really, by the time I noticed he had it out, he was putting it back in his pocket."

"He wasn't an FBI agent. In fact, I don't think he was any kind of federal agent at all. I think he was a fake."

"But he had that badge, I mean, you just said so yourself."

"Just 'cause he had a badge in his pocket doesn't make him a federal agent. Besides, I got a quick look at the thing. It said something like Office of Personnel Management. They aren't investigating gambling. And even if they were, wouldn't the Nevada Gaming Commission be looking into something if it wasn't right? Those jerks were faking it."

"But why? And if they were faking it, how'd they know about your pal Tubby Gustafson? It sounded to me like they had some pretty up-to-date information."

"Yeah, I don't get that part yet. Something's up. I just can't figure out what."

Twenty-one

It had been dark for quite some time before a car finally stopped. Actually, it was a taxi. We waved our arms and jumped up and down to get his attention. He slowed and studied us for a long moment. It must have been a slow night because he eventually stopped and let us climb in.

"Oh, man, thanks for stopping," I said as the wonderful air conditioning enveloped me.

"Car break down?" he asked.

"Not exactly," I said.

"We've been walking for hours. Hotter than hell out there. I think I could drain an entire barrel of beer at this point," Goose said.

"Sounds like a good idea on just about any night. Where are you two headed?"

"The Bellagio," I said, then caught the driver studying us in his rearview mirror.

"Be a good fifteen minutes 'fore we get there," he said and headed down the road.

"Man, I'm thinking I might make use of that Jacuzzi in your room while you're running Barbie's luggage over to her," Goose said.

"I think at this stage she can just go the night without her damn luggage. I'm too tired to get it over to her. Let her fend for herself, might serve her right."

"You want to live that close to the edge?"

"Hey, I already told you, she basically dumped me during our little chat in the shower room. And now I'm supposed to jump through hoops? What's wrong with this picture? You go ahead and grab the Jacuzzi. I'll be in the shower, and there's a pretty good chance I might be sipping a beverage or two once we get into the room."

We drove on in silence, past the airport, and onto streets with sidewalks, where the buildings quickly began to grow taller. Suddenly, the Bellagio was up ahead, and I felt as if it was one of the more welcome sights I'd had in my life.

I paid the driver, gave him an extra tip for picking us up, and we walked into the air-conditioned comfort of the hotel. The security guard was in the process of triple-checking my magnetic room key when he noticed Goose walking up behind me and waved us through to the elevators. As soon as I stepped into the room, I began to unbutton the Barbie shirt. I had it off by the time I was standing in front of the refrigerator behind the bar.

"How's a beer sound, Goose?"

"Only one?"

"Only one at a time. Hey, use your employee discount and see if you can get a dozen more up here, there's only six in the refrigerator."

"What kind are they?"

"What kind? Goose, they're cold, what more do you need to know?"

He phoned room service and ordered a dozen more beers. They arrived about thirty minutes later, neither one of us had begun to get cleaned up yet. Instead, we'd both fallen asleep on our respective couches after finishing a beer and a half. Room service knocking on the door woke us up. I pretended I was still asleep and let Goose deal with the charge and the tip.

"Thanks, Francie," he said, closing the door. He carried a large ice bucket across the room and set it on the bar.

I heard him pop the cap off a bottle and pretended to wake up by groaning and stretching.

"Oh, so now you're awake?"

"Yeah, I'll take one of those if you don't mind."

"Here," he said, then set his bottle on the bar and unbuckled his belt. "I think I'm going to finish this in the Jacuzzi if that's alright with you."

"Fine, I'm going to hit the shower. See you in thirty minutes," I said and headed for another bathroom.

* * *

"So how in the hell did Kenny end up out here?" I asked Goose. We were sitting on opposite couches with our feet up on the coffee table. We were each wearing a white terrycloth robe emblazoned with the Bellagio logo and drinking a beer.

"Kenny was working for the Department of Trans-portation at home. There was some office incident, I'm not sure what, exactly. Anyway, he was laid off, and the next thing you know, my mom got a postcard from him. One week later I'm sent out to bring him home, but, to tell you the truth, he's happy here. I guess they like the work he's doing, whatever that is. They pay him, he's employed, making enough to live on, and now I like it out here, too. I've been here for over a year and a half. That's longer than I've been anywhere since we got home from our deployment. So we're going to stay, or at least we were planning to until those three jerks washed up on shore. You call your contact back in St. Paul?"

"You mean Tubby? Yeah, he never answers. I left a message, then called his right-hand man, Fat Freddy Zimmermann."

"What's the plan?"

"Plan? I got no idea. I'll see if Tubby or Freddy have any info on those three guys. Hopefully, get a feel for what Tubby is involved in out here, see if that maybe gives me an idea of what's going on."

"Any idea on the other front?" Goose asked, then drained the rest of his beer and stood up.

"You mean Barbie? I'll get her luggage over to her tomorrow morning and play it by ear. Hopefully, she's had the night to dial down and come to her senses, guess I'll have to see."

Twenty-two

My first thought when I woke the following morning was Morton. We'd arrived at the Bellagio too late last night to get Morton and Sugar out of the Groom Room. So I quickly got dressed and hurried down to the lower level to get them, feeling just a little more guilty with every step.

Ramona, the same girl as when I dropped them off yesterday, was behind the counter and greeted me with a smile. "Oh, hi, did you have a nice evening?" If she noticed my windburned face, she didn't react.

"It was… interesting. Sorry I didn't make it back in time to get them."

"Oh, not to worry, they had a great time. We have an indoor courtyard where they can chase balls and run until they're tired. They must have missed one another. The Golden Retriever was in the same kennel as the little one when I came in this morning."

"Really?"

"Yeah, he must have jumped the fence. We gave them each a bath this morning, so they're all clean and brushed."

"Can I charge this to my room?"

"Of course." She ran her fingers across the keypad on her desk a couple of times, and a moment later, a printer fired up and spit out a receipt. She handed the receipt to me and said, "Just sign that on the line at the bottom while I go get them."

She was back in the office just a minute later with Morton and Sugar. Morton's tail was going a mile a minute, and Sugar hopped back and forth and barked when they saw me.

"They're really excited to see you," Ramona laughed, then handed their leashes over to me. She bent down and gave both of them a rub behind the ear and a little hug. "You come back and see us again real soon."

I thanked her, and we took the elevator back up to the room. I unclipped their leashes as soon as we were inside the door, and they both took off and jumped on Goose, still asleep on the couch.

"Aw, God, what the hell are you doing?" he groaned.

"Come on, Goose, rise, and shine."

Morton's tail knocked a couple of empty beer bottles off the coffee table as Goose sat up, rubbed his eyes, and groaned some more.

"What the hell time is it?"

"It's damn near noon."

"Noon! I'm supposed to be at work. I gotta fly, man," he said, jumping off the couch and heading for the bathroom.

"Hey, Goose, come on. Who's gonna watch Morton while I bring Barbie's luggage and Sugar over to her?"

"He'll be okay. Besides," he called from the bathroom, "you'll only be gone for about an hour, right?"

"Not if she realizes the error of her ways."

"Barbie?"

"Yeah."

"I don't want to be the one to burst your bubble, man," he said, pulling on his jeans as he stepped out of the bathroom. "But you might want to be prepared for her to still be all wrapped up in that Barbie routine. Maybe give her some space, you know, let her do her thing for a couple of days, get it out of her system, and then she'll be back to normal… whatever that is."

"You know what this joint is costing me a day," I indicated the room with a sweep of my hand. "And she's the one who booked it."

"I know, I know, Dev. Look, she's obsessed with the whole Barbie deal. But you knew that before you got on the plane with her, right?"

"Well, yeah, kind of, I suppose."

"I'm just suggesting if you pressure her now, while she's living the dream, it's probably not going to go your way. That's all I'm saying. Hey, you seen my shirt? I think I'm already late."

"It's at the end of the couch, Sugar's lying on it," I said, then walked into the bedroom and started cramming clothes none too carefully into one of Barbie's pink suitcases.

"Thanks, man. Let's touch base tonight. I'm off at seven. I'll give you a call, okay?"

"Yeah." I was in the process of pulling pink outfits off of their hangers and cramming them into a suitcase.

"Is all that going to fit in there?"

"Really not my problem, now, is it?"

"Okay, good luck with that," Goose said and hurried out of the room.

I grabbed Barbie's makeup bag, the shiny black thing big enough to hide a small child, walked into the bathroom, and began tossing makeup, lipsticks, brushes, and creams into the bag. I'm pretty sure one of the cream containers had the lid off when I tossed it into the bag, but I really didn't care.

I clipped the leash onto Sugar's collar, slung the makeup bag over my shoulder, grabbed a pink suitcase in each hand, and headed out the door. Morton was chewing on something pink as I left, and I didn't want to interrupt him. He raised his head as I opened the door but never got off the couch to follow me.

Twenty-three

There were only a couple of people in line for taxis, and the guy directing people kept a straight face when he looked at me with two pink suitcases, a makeup bag, and a fuzzy little sixteen-ounce dog on a pink leash. "Where you headed, sir?"

"The Palms," I said, and Sugar barked.

He opened the passenger door for me, then grabbed one of the suitcases, and tossed it into the trunk. I threw the other suitcase and the makeup bag in on top of it and slammed the trunk closed.

"Enjoy your day, sir," he said as I took a five-dollar bill out of my pocket and handed it to him.

"The Palms?" the driver said as Sugar and I slid into the back seat.

"That's right."

He sped off into traffic, looked at me a half-dozen times in the rearview mirror, and finally said, "You part of that big deal they got going on over there today?"

"What?"

"Oh, sorry, thought you might be part of a big photoshoot going on at The Palms, no offense, I just saw the pink suitcases and the dog. You know, I'm thinking my two girls and their Barbie dolls. I guess it's some new marketing campaign they're doing. It was all over the news this morning, drawing quite the crowd. I dropped a couple of ladies off about an hour ago, and the place was jammed."

"A Barbie photoshoot?"

"Yeah, that's what they said. You didn't know anything about it?" he said in a tone that suggested I was really nuts if I was wandering around town with all that pink stuff and a little white dog.

"See, what did I tell you," he said five minutes later. We were still a block and a half from The Palms, inching forward in a line of traffic that, for all practical purposes, wasn't moving.

"You gotta be kidding me. Is there another way in that place?"

"It's the Barbie shoot, God, talk about nuts. Let's see, another way. You know, there is, if you don't mind slipping in the workers' entrance."

"No, actually, I'd prefer that. The fewer people that see me, the better, as far as I'm concerned."

"Okay. Let me just zip around the block here, and you can hop out. The less time I have to spend in this jam, the better."

We waited for two stoplights going around the block, but he eventually got us there. A set of double doors marked 'Employees Only' were propped wide open, and four guys were wheeling a number of carts loaded with boxes through the doors. I paid the fare, gave him a tip, then pulled the pink suitcases and the makeup bag out of the trunk. With all the activity, Sugar stayed close to me, and we made it to a bank of service elevators in just a couple of minutes. Mercifully, the elevator went to the top of the building. I pushed the button for the twenty-sixth floor and prayed no one else stepped on.

Sugar and I stepped out on the twenty-sixth floor and then walked about two miles along a series of plush hallways before we finally reached the Barbie suite. I knocked on the door and waited. I was just about to leave the luggage at the door and take Sugar with me when the door opened.

"Yes? Oh, hi, hey, sorry, I've already forgotten your name, I'm Camille," she said and extended her hand. She looked at the suitcases and said, "We've been wondering, come on in." She grabbed one of the pink suitcases and wheeled it into the suite. I followed with the other suitcase, the makeup bag, and Sugar. As Camille wheeled the suitcase ahead of me, I noticed a pink sleeve hanging out of the side.

"Barbie, looks who's finally here," Camille said.

Barbie was seated in a makeup chair with her eyes closed, and a large green cloth draped over her. Two women were fidgeting around her. One held a large makeup brush, and the other had a spritz bottle she was squirting into Barbie's hair. A third woman was working on her nails. Barbie's feet were bare, and she had cotton balls wedged between each toe, her toenails were pink with a white stripe on the end of each nail.

Kenny sat in a chair opposite Barbie with a small white bib around his neck. Some guy was brushing makeup on his face and gave me a look that suggested, 'How dare I interrupt.'

Barbie opened her eyes at the sound of Camille's voice and focused on Sugar. "Oh, baby," she screamed and sat upright. Sugar strained at her leash, so I let her go, and she hopped onto Barbie's lap, then turned and gave me a look as if to say 'Look where I get to go.'

"How's it going, Barbie?"

"Oh, Dev, what took you? I expected all this yesterday evening."

"Sorry about that, we ran into a little complication."

"We?"

"Goose and I, you see he—"

"Spare me, please. Okay, thanks for bringing everything over, I guess. I've got to get ready for the photoshoot, they've moved everything up a day," she closed her eyes and settled back into her chair.

"Yeah," I said, "The cab driver was telling me about it. I guess it was advertised. There was a line of cars a block long just to get into this place. We had to—"

"Really?" she said and sat upright, looking all excited.

"We didn't actually advertise the photoshoot," Camille said. "More of a guerrilla marketing technique. What we did was leak a memo to the press, and they spread the word, thinking they're in on the top-secret stuff. It's a great promo gimmick, doesn't cost us a thing, and there's a fifty-fifty shot it will be picked up by Google or Yahoo or someone and go viral."

"Oh my God. Okay, Dev, you have to leave, I want to look perfect," Barbie said, then settled back in her chair and closed her eyes. The three women clustered around her went back to work.

"Come on, I'll let you out," Camille said and headed for the door.

"Did you enjoy your night here?" I asked Barbie.

"Hello. Dev, working, I'm getting ready for the photoshoot," she said, not bothering to open her eyes.

"Come on, Dev," Camille called.

"Nice talking to you, Kenny," I called. He lifted his hand and waved.

I was almost at the door when Barbie called, "Did you remember to pack my shoes, the pink ones with the gold toe caps?"

"Not to worry, we've got dozens of pairs she can choose from, thanks, see you," Camille said, then half-pushed me out of the room and closed the door behind me.

I was standing out in the hall, wondering what in the hell had just happened. I was tempted to knock on the door again, no, make that pound and then kick it in, but then what? I headed for elevators and rode down to the main floor.

Twenty-four

I stepped out of the elevator, walked to the closest bar I could see, and ordered a beer. I conjured up an image of Barbie flitting around the casino getting her picture taken, and I'd suddenly show up drunk and create a scene, maybe throw up on her or fling a deck of cards at her or…

Two of them walked past, not twenty feet from me. Fortunately, they didn't see me. The big guy with the shaved head and the one who had flashed the fake badge at me while Goose and I were sitting in the back of that van yesterday. I debated finishing my beer for a half-second, then threw a ten-dollar bill on the bar, took a quick swallow, and headed out the door behind them.

I thought they were going to get in line for a taxi, but instead, they walked past the taxi line and headed down the entrance drive. They seemed to be involved in a conversation and completely unaware I was following. They continued on that way for another two blocks. I kept maybe fifty yards behind them until they took a quick left down an alley. I hurried to the alley and watched as they took a right between two buildings. I was debating whether to follow when I heard an engine start up, and in the next instant, the black hood of that van appeared. I stepped back into the doorway of the building and watched as they drove past, repeating the license number as they headed down the street. A taxi suddenly pulled around the corner and stopped to let a couple out. I ran toward him, and the couple jumped back in fear, thinking I was a mugger or something.

"Sorry, didn't mean to frighten you. Just wanted to grab this taxi."

"Sure thing," the guy said, not sounding all that sure.

"You in a hurry, buddy?" The driver said as I hopped into the back of the cab.

"You see that black van about a block and a half ahead, can you follow him, please?"

"Someone owe you money or hitting on your girl-friend?" he asked as he accelerated down the street. Up ahead, the van put it's right blinker on, slowed for half a second, then turned.

"Just some guys I know, I want to see what they're up to."

He gave me a quick glance in the rearview mirror.

"We're always playing practical jokes on one an-other. If I can get a home address, I can send them a fake letter from the IRS, it'll drive them crazy."

"Yeah," he said, then turned right at the corner and sped up. We followed them for another ten minutes, deeper and deeper into a residential area. "This is Hen-derson," the driver said, turning onto a side street. The area looked like a development that couldn't be more than about ten or fifteen years old. The houses all appeared to be pretty much the same, a driveway leading up to a double car garage with a house tacked on behind it. All the structures had brick fronts and white stucco sides with a tiled roof. More than a few 'For Sale' signs were posted up and down the street.

The yards, such as they were, consisted of red dirt, gravel, and the occasional scraggly weed, not unlike the no-man's land Goose and I were dropped off in yesterday evening. On the other hand, no one had to take time to cut the grass, because there wasn't any. The taxi slowed at the corner.

"Everything okay?"

"Yeah, I know this area, former girlfriend lives on the next street over. My guess is they'll be pulling into a driveway. Thought I'd maybe give them a minute to park, get out of the car and go inside before we drove past. No sense in calling attention to ourselves. You know, wouldn't want to spoil your practical joke," he said, sounding like he didn't believe my earlier explanation.

We waited another half-minute, then he turned onto the street, Spur Cross Circle, and continued down. The houses here were still white stucco with the tile roof and brick front and seemed to look exactly the same on either side of the street, but the garages on this street were tucked under the second floor of the house and roofs were at an angle rather than peaked.

"There they are, see 'em?" the driver said, pointing down the road. The black van was pulled into the driveway and parked up against the garage door. A 'For Sale' sign was posted in the front yard, as well as in the yards on either side. As we drew closer, a hint of red stood out alongside the van. The red pickup truck from yesterday became apparent as we drove past.

"You get that address?"

"The address? Oh, damn it, I was so focused on the van and that pickup, I forgot. Can we go past again?"

"It's number twenty, address was on the garage. Here," he said and handed a pen over his shoulder. I wrote the address down on the edge of a dollar bill, then handed the pen back over his shoulder.

"Afraid I can't help you with the zip code over here," he said, then tossed the pen onto the front passenger seat.

"You can take me to the Bellagio, I guess."

"Bellagio it is," he said, and the taxi seemed to pick up a little speed as we rounded a curve in the road.

"Let me ask you something. I'm a tourist, not familiar with the town."

"Oh, really?"

"Yeah, this a nice area?"

"Henderson? Yeah, it's pretty nice, second biggest city in the state, Vegas is the biggest, of course. Population is something like two seventy, maybe three hundred thousand. I mean, like everywhere out here, it took a hit in that whole subprime mortgage fiasco. Still haven't completely recovered."

"That why there's so many for sale signs?"

"That's part of it. Funny thing is, the prices seem to be going up even though more and more places seem to be going on the market. This here is a pretty nice area, a couple blocks over, you got places going for over a million bucks. Places around here," he slowed and put his blinker on, waited for two cars to pass, then sped up once he pulled onto the four-lane road. "Places around here, like the one where your *pals* are," he emphasized the word 'pals,' suggesting anything but. "Place like that probably goes for two seventy-five maybe three-fifty, depending. They got a pool, maybe a couple of bathrooms, you know, it all adds up. You can check the place out online. Just Google the address. God, nowadays you can have a tour of the place and never leave your own home."

"Let me ask you one more thing, the state gaming commission, what do you know about them?"

"The gaming commission? At one time, they were more or less influenced by the mob, if not run by it. Honestly, the sense I get is they've been pretty straight shooters at least for the past quarter of a century. There's too much at stake here to have people thinking the games are rigged. You know, just about everyone who comes to this town will tell you that they won. And they probably did, they just forget to mention the fact that they lost it all before they left. Are the games rigged? No, not really.

The odds are just stacked so that if you keep at it long enough, eventually you'll probably lose, that's all. Hey, here's the Bellagio, it's been real, man."

Twenty-five

Morton was asleep on the couch when I opened the door. The chewed remnants of Barbie's thong lay scattered on the carpet around him. It figured, Morton took a nap and was getting more action than me. I grabbed his leash, and we headed out the door for a quick walk, the temperature was forecast for 107 today. It was already beastly hot and still had a ways to go, so our walk was short and sweet. Once back in the Bellagio, I took Morton down to the Groom Room.

Ramona was sitting at the front counter reading a book. She smiled when we came in and hopped out of her chair. "Back for more, are we?"

Morton's tail fired up, and he rushed toward her.

"It's just so hot outside, I was going to take him for a walk, but he's just not used to these temps. Neither am I, for that matter."

"Who can get used to the heat?" she said, bending down to rub Morton behind the ear. He licked her face a couple of times, definitely getting more action than me.

"I was wondering if I could leave him with you? Hoping you could have him chase those tennis balls, give him some exercise."

"Sure we can. The little dog?"

"Sugar."

"Oh, that's cute. You know that was Barbie's dog's name?"

"Please don't remind me. She's a star today, she's doing a photoshoot over at The Palms, with Barbie."

"Oh, you're kidding, I caught something about that online. I was thinking I'd maybe go over there once my shift was done."

"You're a Barbie fan?"

She looked at me like I was crazy. "Who isn't?" I couldn't see any point in voicing my opinion.

"How's Sugar doing?"

"Doing, fine, I guess. Like I said, she's going to be a part of that photoshoot, I think. She's a little dog. You know how they can be, sort of hyper sometimes."

"Actually, I meant after last night, you know . . ."

"Last night? What, she didn't sleep well?"

"No, she, ahh, had company," Romana said, then stared at Morton.

"Yeah, you said he jumped the fence. He did that once before at home. Actually, some dog was in heat. Anyway, they banned him, well, us, from the kennel, for life. I always thought he was a dog after my own— Wait, is that why he ended up in her kennel? Sugar was—"

"Sorry," Romana said. "I reported it to management. They've got someone coming out later in the week to make the fences two feet higher. We've never seen anything like it, I mean, we've never had a problem in the four and a half years we've been operating."

I looked down at Morton. He was definitely getting more action than me. "I'll be back to pick him up before you close."

"Not to worry, he's the only one here today, so it's safe."

"Thanks, Ramona," I said, then left Morton in her trusted care. His tail was still wagging as I left. He didn't even turn to watch me go out the door. I wondered what I was going to tell Barbie. I wondered if I should tell Barbie. How could Sugar even handle Morton?

I took the elevator up to the main floor and made my way to the Avis desk.

"I'd like to rent a car for the day."

"Certainly, sightseeing?"

"Yes, just wanted to drive around off the strip and see the city, I'm thinking of purchasing some property," I lied.

I got a tour of the city via the four different maps she gave me. A list of a half-dozen out-of-the-way places to grab dinner, two areas that she circled in red on the maps that I should stay away from. "We're open twenty-four hours, seven days a week, so enjoy your drive," she said and handed me the keys.

I studied the maps for a couple of minutes in the front seat of the silver Ford Fusion. I took some time to get somewhat familiar with the dash, and then headed back toward Henderson. I made a number of wrong turns, and it took me twice as long as the taxi yesterday, but I finally found Spur Cross Circle again. As I turned onto the street, I looked ahead, and the driveway appeared to be empty. I drove past, trying to see if there was any movement inside, which was a waste of time because the drapes were drawn, and the shades were pulled. I drove to the end of the block, made a U-turn, and parked across the street from number twenty.

The garage doors were windowless, so there was no way to determine if a vehicle was in the garage. I walked up to the front door, pushed the doorbell, and began to wonder what I would say if someone opened the door. I heard it ring inside. I pushed the doorbell three times, but no one ever came to the door. I noticed there was mail in the mailbox. Unfortunately, it was just two circulars, both addressed to resident. There was a path along the brick wall on the right side of the house that extended into the back. A wrought-iron gate led into the backyard. I walked around to the side, the gate was unlocked, so I strolled into the backyard.

The area consisted of a poured concrete path with a swimming pool rising maybe six inches above the pathway in the center of the small walled area. From the look of things, the pool had been drained some time ago, and there was nothing to indicate recent habitation. No chairs, no tables, no grill, nothing, not so much as a beer bottle. I did spot a pile of maybe a dozen cigarette butts along the far edge of the pool area and smudges on the concrete path where the cigarettes had been ground out.

There was a sliding glass door that led into the house. I glanced in the door, couldn't spot anything that suggested life and cautiously pulled at the door, it slid open. I cocked an ear and listened but didn't hear anything, so I stepped inside and quietly slid the door closed behind me. There wasn't so much as a clock ticking.

I walked through the kitchen and peeked into the dining area, empty. Same thing with the adjoining living room. The shades were down, the curtains pulled and not so much as a stick of furniture. I went back to the kitchen and started poking around. The cabinets were empty, five cans of beer still in the plastic holder sat on the kitchen counter next to the refrigerator. I opened the refrigerator door, and the light didn't come on. There was nothing in the refrigerator and not so much as a spoon or a paper towel anywhere in the kitchen. I opened the door to the attached garage. It was empty except for a sheet of cardboard left on the floor to catch an oil drip. I flicked the light switch a couple of times, but no lights came on. The power to the house was turned off.

I climbed up the stairs to the second floor. There were four bedrooms. One was empty. The other three had sleeping bags and suitcases open on the floor. The bathroom had a roll of toilet paper sitting on the vanity and just the empty cardboard roll in the toilet paper holder, no soap, no razors or toothbrushes. I went back into the first bedroom, checked the suitcase for anything with a name or some form of identification, there wasn't one. I did find a pistol clip loaded with nine-millimeter rounds. In the next bedroom, the clothes in the suitcase smelled heavily of cigarette smoke. Along with dirty laundry, the suitcase held a half-empty carton of Marlboro cigarettes. There was a Delta airlines name tag on the handle of the suitcase with the name Paulo Caputo.

The third bedroom had an empty can of beer on the floor next to the sleeping bag. A pile of dirty clothes were tossed in the corner of the room, the t-shirt with 'Black Olives Matter' was wadded up on the top of the pile and looked like it had been tossed from across the room. A copy of *Treats!,* a classy porn magazine, if there is such a thing, lay on the carpet next to the sleeping bag.

One thing seemed pretty clear. They weren't federal agents. I took out my phone and sent a text message to Fat Freddy Zimmerman and Tubby Gustafson.

'Does the name Paulo Caputo mean anything to you? He is running in Las Vegas with someone named Danny who has a scar across the tip of his nose and a large guy with a shaved head. Caputo seemed to know about you and was aware you visited my office a few days ago. He seems to be staying in a vacant house in Henderson, NV, Address: 20 Spur Cross Road. Would appreciate an answer. Haskell'

I was tempted to take the beer from the kitchen counter but left it. I climbed in my car and drove up the street. On the way, I counted seven more homes for sale on just that one street. Including the one I'd just been in and the ones on either side of that structure, it made ten for sale on just one street.

I hadn't made it halfway back to the Bellagio when my phone rang. By the time I pulled over and turned the car off, whoever was calling had hung up. I redialed and waited.

Twenty-six

When Tubby Gustafson answered he didn't sound happy. "Now you're too busy to take my call?"

"No, sir. I was driving. I didn't want to get in an accident, and I wanted to be sure I was paying complete attention to you when we talked."

"So, all of a sudden, you're not driving?"

"I pulled off the road, sir."

"Mmm-mmm," he growled. "How'd you meet up with that bastard Caputo kid?"

Interesting he said 'kid.' It suggested there was a father or uncle involved somewhere and, with that, the danger of connections.

"He was following me around. Actually, following my pal's younger brother, and that was the original reason my pal, Goose, asked me to come out here to Vegas."

"I thought you were out there because that little cutie was doing the photoshoot?"

How the hell did he know about that? "No, sir, that just kind of happened. In fact, if I knew then what I know now, I wouldn't have brought her out here. Anyway, those three guys were following us around, and they finally cornered a cab we were in, me and Goose. Put us in the back of the van and drove us out to the middle of nowhere and made us walk back in a hundred-and-ten-degree heat."

"You tell them anything?"

"I don't have anything to tell. Like I said in my text message, they knew you and Freddy were in my office the other day. In fact, they thought I worked for you, sir, and…"

"God, as if my days aren't long enough…"

"They knew that my pal's brother worked at The Palms."

"What's this brother business?"

"My pal Goose, actually, his name is Arthur Gander, and his brother—"

"Kenny Gander is his brother? The one they call Rain Man?"

"I don't know anything about that, sir. I just know his brother Kenny is doing something with numbers and percentages at The Palms."

"And Caputo and these other two clowns were interested?"

"Yeah, they told us they were federal agents, and they've been trying to become friends with Kenny. That's the whole reason I came out here, well, and because you suggested it might be a good idea, " I said, covering myself. "Goose didn't like the looks of them, and neither one of us believed they were federal agents."

"And they're trying to get close to Kenny?"

"Yeah, the whole thing is kind of screwy, if you ask me. We couldn't figure out why they didn't just pick up the phone and call him or give him an ice cream cone."

"How much longer were you planning to be out there?"

"Another day and a half, sir," I said, figuring that would get me off the hook.

"That should be more than enough time to bring this to a conclusion, Haskell. You're not to let Caputo anywhere near Kenny, and I expect you to keep me posted. I want an immediate report if and when something happens."

"But I don't have any idea what…hello? Hello? Mr. Gustafson?" Oh, just great. He'd hung up, and I didn't have the slightest idea what he wanted, what I was supposed to look for, or what I was supposed to call him about.

Don't let them near Kenny? What the hell did that mean? As far as I knew, the guy was locked in a room looking at numbers, at least when he wasn't getting his makeup done with Barbie. And what's with Tubby's offer, what's that about?

As soon as I got back to my room, I placed a call to Goose, ended up leaving a message, then switched on my laptop and Googled Paulo Caputo. There were a couple of guys with the same name, none of whom remotely fit the description of the guy I was looking for. Just for fun, I googled Kenny and came up empty-handed. I kept wondering, what was supposed to happen in the next day and a half?

Twenty-seven

The Palms was mobbed. Apparently, it was the place to be this afternoon, at least based on the number of people crammed into the casino watching the Barbie photoshoot. I stood about a half-mile back in the crowd and could just barely make out Barbie and Kenny seated at a table under the lights with a half-dozen cameras going. That didn't count the hundred or so cell phones held high in the air flashing their own shots. God, the two of them, Barbie and Kenny, they'd be lucky if they didn't wake up with PTSD tomorrow morning, given the non-stop flashing.

The crowd cheered, apparently because Barbie had just won at whatever game they were playing. The only way I knew she won was I could see her jump up and down, clap her hands a half dozen times, squeal and then plant a not-too-casual kiss on Kenny's lips.

I looked around the crowd as best I could but couldn't see anyone resembling Paulo Caputo or his pals. I guess that was good news. I sent Goose a text message telling him where I was and to get in touch with me when he was done working.

More cheering and flashes erupted from the crowd as I began to wiggle my way toward the front. As I drew closer to Barbie, I lost count of the dirty looks I received from women holding their cell phones over their heads. More than a few of them were dressed in Barbie outfits.

It took close to twenty minutes, but I made it up to the front where there was a pink velvet rope draped across the aisle and three rather large security guards. "I'm sorry, sir, would you happen to have a VIP pass?" one of the guards asked, knowing full well what my answer would be.

"A VIP pass? That's my girlfriend up there," I said and pointed to Barbie. I didn't feel the need to add the prefix 'ex.'

He looked at me and then at the guard next to him, who shook his head 'no.' "Afraid you may have made a mistake, sir."

"No, really, that's Barbie Dahl, she's staying in the Barbie suite. That's her dog, Sugar, she's holding, and that's Kenny seated next to her."

"Ken," the guard corrected.

"He works here, at The Palms, figures out numbers and percentages or something. Lives with his brother. This is the first day of the photoshoot, and a guy named Tom Diamond is in marketing or something for The Palms, and he set all this up. I was there yesterday, in the Barbie suite. A lady named Camille was his assistant."

The two guards looked at one another, conferred with the third guard, then the one I initially talked to said,

"Wait here a minute." He waded through the VIP crowd, and I lost sight of him. He came back about five minutes later carrying Sugar. "Your name, Hassle?"

"That's right," I said, not willing to deal with making a correction.

"Yeah, I guess the dog needs to be taken outside." He passed Sugar to me over the pink velvet rope. "Here, you can use this to clean up after her," he said and handed me a blue plastic bag.

"Huh?"

"The dog, obviously, we can't have her going in here," he said, then glanced around to indicate the crowd of Barbie fans. A number of women standing around us started flashing their cell phones taking pictures of Sugar, which seemed to cause her to curl deeper into my arms. "Bring her back when she's finished. Okay?" the guard called after me as I turned to make our way through the crowd.

I pushed our way through the mob toward the entrance. The flashing cellphones slowed down, but there were still people taking pictures as we headed out the door. Sugar had her pink leash attached, and I set her down on the sidewalk and headed toward the street. About halfway to the street, she stopped and assumed the position. Then I stood there hanging onto her leash while she did her business. I carried on an internal argument regarding whether or not to pick up after her. Responsibility won the day, and I deposited the blue plastic bag in a trash container next to the front door as we made our way back into the casino.

I repeated the procedure of snaking our way through the crowd up toward the front. Only this time, when someone gave me a dirty look, I smiled and said, "I have to get Sugar up there for some pictures." We made it up to the front in half the time.

The same security guard looked at me and then Sugar.

"Mind if I bring her back up to Barbie? I want to be sure she takes her meds."

"You mean Barbie's popping pills?" he asked and flashed an evil grin.

"No, Sugar, she's on a strict regime. You can take her up, I guess, but if some problem develops or Barbie forgets to give her the pills, well," I glanced at his name tag. "Well, Tim, it's your neck, not mine."

He seemed to think about that for a half-second, then unhooked the pink velvet rope and let us into the VIP section. "I'm guessing you can find your way from here?"

"Yeah, I can see her right up there," I said just as the crowd erupted, and Barbie squealed, jumped up and down and clapped her hands.

"Barbie, hey Barbie," I called as we neared the front. She gave me a sideways glance while she firmly planted her lips on Kenny's. She held her lips there for a long moment staring at me wide-eyed, then said, "Dev, how did *you* get in here?"

"I did what I always do, I lied," I said, then handed Sugar to her.

"Did she do her business?"

"Yeah, I was…"

"Okay, thanks," she said, then quickly turned away from me. My first thought was to kick her in the butt. Instead, I called, "How's it going, Kenny?"

"Hey, Dev. This is really crazy, they've taken over two thousand three hundred and fifty-seven photos." He said just as a couple more cameras went off. "Make that two-thousand three hundred and sixty-one, I think. But I'm not sure because, with all the noise and cheering, it's really hard to hear the cameras click, you know?" ·

"You're having a good time, Kenny?" He had lipstick smears on both cheeks.

"Yeah, although I keep thinking when this is done, I'm going to have a lot of spreadsheets stacked up on my desk just waiting for me to go over them."

"You just enjoy yourself and have fun, you take care of Barbie, okay?"

"I will," he smiled at the floor.

The dealer dealt another card to Barbie, and she turned and looked at Kenny. He shook his head 'no,' the dealer gave himself a card, and Barbie squealed as the crowd erupted.

"She's on an eighty-seven percent winning streak, that's almost impossible. I guess it's just Barbie luck," Kenny said.

"You keep an eye on her, you'll know when it's time to quit."

"Sixty-one percent is the safe cutoff."

"You're the boss, Kenny. No one knows it like you do." I looked at the stack of chips Barbie had accumulated playing blackjack. It had to be another forty or fifty grand. Unbelievable. I scanned across the room, and suddenly, there in the crowd was Paulo Caputo. The big guy with the shaved head was standing next to him. He saw me, said something to Paulo, and they both quickly faded from view.

"You're going to stay right here, Kenny?"

"Yeah, we have to for at least another half-hour, then back up to the Barbie suite. I get to be in a lot of the photos. I guess I look like Ken, kind of." He leaned in next to me just as Barbie was dealt a ten and whispered, "It's really been fun, I think she might like me."

"Who can blame her, Kenny? You've always been a great guy."

"Ken, dear, you're not paying attention," Barbie said. "Oh, Dev, you're still here? Thanks for helping with Sugar, but she should be fine now. Ken, he dealt me a ten, what do I do?"

"Double down, remember? I showed you how."

Barbie nodded, smiled, then faced the dealer and said something. He dealt her two cards, and she shrugged and squealed. "Look what he gave me, a four and a seven."

I turned and made my way through the crowd. A minute later, there was a loud cheer, and sure enough, Barbie was clapping and then wrapped her arms around Ken's neck and planted another kiss.

Twenty-eight

There was probably no point in attempting to follow Paulo Caputo, but I made my way over to that side of the room anyway. I looked around for another fifteen minutes scanning the crowd but never saw him, then headed for one of the bars and ordered a beer. Goose phoned me a few minutes later.

"Where are you?"

"I'm over at The Palms," I told him about the photoshoot, the crowd, the fact that I'd caught a glimpse of Paulo Caputo. "Apparently, Kenny's been giving Barbie pointers on playing blackjack, and she had a pretty decent stack of chips in front of her when I left."

"They're playing cards? I thought craps was her—"

"I think it's part of the whole ad campaign, get shots of them playing all the games. Kenny seems to be enjoying himself, Barbie's winning, and can't seem to get enough of Kenny."

Goose was quiet for a moment, then said, "What's that about? You want me to say something to him?"

"Relax, it's not an issue. Her timing sucked, but then, when is it ever a good time to get dumped?"

"You sure, man? I mean, you're out here helping us, and I certainly didn't mean for Kenny to jump in and—"

"Don't worry about it, it's not his fault. Hey, I got a call from Tubby this afternoon."

"Everything okay? What kind of trouble are you in now?"

"None, at least that I know of. He asked when I was leaving, and I told him day after tomorrow, and he said that should work out fine, as long as I kept Paulo Caputo away from Kenny. You aware of anything happening here in the next day and a half?"

"At The Palms, no, nothing. Well, except I think they're going to be doing more of that photoshoot. Kenny told me some of it will be in the Barbie suite, and then a couple of times, they'll bring the two of them down to the casino for twenty minutes or so, just to get folks all stirred up."

"I can't figure out what it is, but we must be missing something."

"There's a big stakes blackjack tournament there tomorrow night, but Kenny doesn't have anything to do with that."

"Blackjack tournament?"

"Heavy hitters from all over the country. They pay a pretty hefty fee. There's a bunch of elimination rounds, you know the gig. I think they do it maybe four times a year, more PR than anything else, and, like I said, Kenny's not involved."

"Would he normally be at something like that?"

"No, I don't think he's ever been at one of those. He's pretty private, doesn't like crowds. Tell you the truth, I'm more than a little surprised he's enjoying that photoshoot. Usually, he'd rather just stay home and watch the Big Lebowski for the millionth time."

"Mmm-mmm, Barbie might be adding a little something extra to the endeavor. Although she'd go ballistic if she knew he liked the Big Lebowski, it's the one movie she can't stand."

"You sure you don't want me to say something to Kenny?"

"Yeah, real sure. As a matter of fact, I'm looking forward to getting back home and just being my boring old self."

"Okay, you're the boss. Any plans for tonight?"

"I'm thinking I might keep an eye on Kenny, make sure that Paulo Caputo guy doesn't get too close. Want to join me?"

"Can we drink on duty?"

"Might be room for a beer or two."

"I gotta finish some things up here. I'll text you when I'm on my way over there."

"See you when I see you," I said and disconnected.

Twenty-nine

It was closer to an hour and a half later before Goose sent me his text message. He must have been watching me when he sent it because he sat down on the barstool next to me less than a minute later.

"I think it's your turn to buy," he said.

"You finally decided to join me."

"Last minute thing, some gal a little over-served, and we had to get her out of the main ladies' room."

"What do you do under those circumstances?"

"Depends on who it is. If she's a guest, we'll take her to her room. If it's a person of note, we have a couple of suites where they can sleep it off. If it's someone who's being a jerk, we got no problem calling the cops and having them hauled away. Fortunately, her husband or boyfriend was waiting for her outside of the ladies' room. In fact, he was the one who called us."

"Waiting for her?"

"She passed out in one of the stalls, we went in to get her and then escorted the two of them up to their room, happens more than you think."

"One of the perks of the job."

"This gal outweighed me by a good seventy-five pounds, no thanks. Anything happening with our gang?"

"If you mean Barbie and your brother, I believe they're still up in the Barbie suite. If you mean your pal, Paulo, I haven't seen him for the past couple of hours. I was hoping you might have an in with whoever is checking the elevators. I was planning to head up to the twenty-sixth floor, but the security guy was only letting people past him if they had a room key, so I just backed off."

"Depends on who they have on duty. Do I get a beer first?"

"If we can travel with it."

We ordered two beers, told the barmaid we were going to walk around, and she put them in plastic cups for us. Goose did know the security guy checking for room keys, so we chatted him up for a minute or two, then waited around the corner in front of the elevator for someone else to show. The elevators have a security feature that requires you to put your key into a slot before you push the button for your floor. We got on with two women close to fifty years old who had spent the better part of the afternoon taking pictures of Barbie. One of them placed her key in the slot and pressed twenty-five. I quickly pressed twenty-six before she removed her key.

"Oh, isn't the Barbie suite on twenty-six?"

"I believe it is."

"We were watching them most of the afternoon, God, I haven't done Barbie for an afternoon in decades."

They both laughed at that and kept laughing until they stepped out of the elevator. We got off on the twenty-sixth floor and headed for the Barbie suite. Fortunately, the hallway was empty.

"I was half-afraid they might have someone posted at the door," Goose said as we approached. He knocked on the door, waited, and when he heard movement from inside the room, he placed his finger over the peephole.

"Who is it?" a voice called from inside.

"Kenny, it's Goose, let me in."

Kenny opened the door and stood there, dripping wet with a large pink bath towel wrapped around him. "Hey, Goose, how's it going?"

"Looks like you're doing better than either one of us," Goose said and stepped into the room.

"Umm, I'm not sure you guys should be here right now," Kenny said, looking over his shoulder, then he followed us into the pink living room. We could hear something gurgling or running in the master bathroom, the Jacuzzi.

"Ken, dear, is everything all right?" Barbie called.

Goose looked at his brother. "Don't tell me you're in the bathtub with her."

Kenny looked at the floor and spoke tonelessly, as if he was reading the back of a direction label. "It's a Jacuzzi, actually. One hundred and four degrees Fahrenheit is the perfect temperature, and twenty minutes is the maximum amount of time to remain in the water."

"Ken, are you getting me another glass of wine?" Barbie called.

"Sounds like you're busy," Goose said. "Want us to help?"

Kenny got a worried look on his face.

"Kenny," I said, "Has anyone tried to get in touch with you, maybe ask to be your friend? Maybe someone named Paul or Paulo or Danny?"

"No, why?"

"I talked to someone who was worried about you. These guys I mentioned aren't nice, and my friend was afraid they might try to take advantage of you."

"Take advantage of me?"

"Ken, I'm waiting," Barbie called. She sounded a little impatient.

"You guys wouldn't let them do that, would you? Take advantage of me how?"

"We don't know how, Kenny. We just want you to be careful. Anyone bothering you or someone you don't know hanging around and acting too friendly. You give us a call, okay?"

"Yeah, I can do that, sure."

"Ken, I'm going to come out there in a minute, you better not be in front of that TV," Barbie called, the joy of the moment seemed to have left her voice.

"Okay, go on back to Barbie and have a good time," I said.

That brought some relief to his face, and he nodded just as Barbie stepped out of the bathroom, wearing only a smile. "Darling didn't you hear me call, I… Dev, what the hell are you doing in here?" she said, then jumped back into the bathroom and peeked around the door frame. "Dev, Sugar is just fine and doesn't need to be taken for a walk. Ken, did you let them in?"

"Take it easy, Barbie, we were in the process of leaving. Kenny was just telling us we had to go," I said, then winked at him.

"Nice seeing you, Barbie," Goose laughed.

"Enjoy the wine," I said as we headed for the door.

"See you, guys," Kenny said and closed the door behind us.

"What in the hell were those two doing in here? Did you let them in?" Barbie shouted from inside the suite.

"You know, I almost feel sorry for him," Goose laughed. "Buy you a beer?"

"That would be nice. Maybe we can figure out my phone conversation with Tubby."

"What do think Kenny's chances are with Barbie tonight?" Goose asked.

"If he gets her that glass of wine, I'd say close to a hundred percent."

Thirty

We headed down the hallway toward the elevators. "I gotta tell you," Goose said. "I only caught a second or two, but that's an awfully nice package Barbie's wrapped in."

"Yeah, she can overcome a lot of negative points with that figure. One time she…"

We spotted the guy with the shaved head first. He came around the corner, saw us at about the same time, and stopped in his tracks.

"What the hell you doing?" Paulo Caputo said as he went to step around him, then stopped and stared at us with his mouth open.

Goose thought before anyone else, raised his wrist to his mouth like he was talking into a radio, and said, "They're up on twenty-six, location alpha. All units converge. Repeat all units converge."

"Shit," Paulo said, and a moment later, the bell rang, signaling an elevator arriving. He turned and took off down the hallway running. The guy with the shaved head snarled and pointed a muscular arm with a fist the size of a ten-pound ham. "You got lucky this time, don't press it," he said, then turned and walked quickly down the hall. He looked over his shoulder a couple of times but kept moving. A moment later, we heard an emergency buzzer begin to sound.

"They took the stairs, that's a security buzzer. They'll have them on camera, come on," Goose said. We hurried down the hall, making sure we didn't go fast enough to catch up with shaved head. We stopped at the door to the staircase. There was a push bar on the door with the warning, '**Emergency Exit ONLY-Alarm Will Sound When Door Is Opened.**' You could hear the alarm doing just that. A door suddenly opened on one of the rooms we'd just passed. A guy stepped out, looked at the two of us, frowned, and quickly went back inside his room.

"You think they're waiting for us?" I asked.

"I think they're probably on the first floor by now heading out of the building," Goose laughed and pushed the door open. Even with the buzzer going, we could hear footsteps echoing off the concrete block walls, and we started down the staircase. We'd covered three flights of stairs, each flight was eight steps to a landing, then another eight steps to the next floor, sixteen steps per floor. The door to each floor had the number written on it in large red letters with a gold shadow. Twenty-six floors, I didn't have to do the math to know I didn't want to follow them all the way down to the ground level.

We could still hear their footsteps echoing off the walls, then the murmur of voices. Someone suddenly shouted, "Haskell, I'm warning you," followed by a gun being fired. The echo from the shot bouncing off the walls seemed to last forever. We heard the footsteps begin again, only this time not so fast. I looked at Goose, indicated heading back up the stairs with a nod of my head, and we turned around and climbed back to the twenty-sixth floor. There was only one problem. The door was locked.

"The damn thing locks automatically. That way, anyone gets in here, they can only exit out the ground floor."

"You mean we have to go all the way down twenty-six floors?"

"Unless you have a better option," Goose said.

"See if you can call someone," I said, pulling out my cellphone. I turned it on and read 'No Service.'

"No service," Goose said, looking at his phone and confirming what I already knew. "Come on, guess we might as well get started."

"That alarm ever stop?" I asked a few minutes later just as the alarm stopped buzzing. "Thank God, I was going to lose what was left of my sanity in another minute if that thing kept on going."

It took us close to fifteen minutes before we reached the ground floor. Thankfully, we didn't meet Paulo Caputo along the way. I pushed the door labeled 'Ground Floor' open and stepped into the loving arms of five security guys. They were dressed all in black with name tags stitched above their left breast pocket. They had tasers, handcuffs, and some other thing hanging from their belts, and they didn't look like the sort of guys you'd want to joke with.

"Enjoy your walk, gentlemen?" a guy with a clipped mustache asked. "We'd appreciate it if you'd come with us, please." His name tag read Donner, and I wondered if he was any relation to the Donner Party, the group who became cannibals in the late eighteen forties.

"Please, let me explain," Goose said. "I work at the Bellagio, my brother is in the Barbie suite with Miss Dahl, he's an employee here, Kenny Gander."

"He's staying with that Barbie chick?" one of the guys asked.

Goose ignored the question. "We were posted outside the suite. We were aware three individuals have been following Miss Dahl and my brother. We saw them here this afternoon during the photoshoot, but lost them in the crowd. Anyway, they were up on twenty-six, saw us and ran. We followed them into the stairway and were in the process of catching them when they fired a round at us. We're unarmed and thought it best if we just let them go."

"So where are they?" another guard asked.

"Probably had someone posted on a floor just in case they had to take the stairs. He'd be ready to open the door and, well, essentially, they got away, probably took the elevator down the rest of the way and just walked out the door. I'm sure you'll have it all on your cameras."

"What's your name?" Donner asked.

"Gander, Arthur Gander, I've been at the Bellagio for the past eighteen months. My boss was in touch with Mr. Manion on your staff just this afternoon. Sent him an image of the man we were chasing, a guy named Paulo Caputo."

"Oh, yeah, they mentioned him in our briefing. And your name?" Donner asked me.

"Devlin Haskell, I'm a licensed private investigator. I accompanied Miss Dahl out here from Minnesota."

"Would you mind coming with us to the office? I just want to get this cleared up. It shouldn't take more than a couple of minutes, don't want the wrong reports getting back to your folks at the Bellagio," Donner smiled, then extended his hand gracefully, and we moved as one with the security guys surrounding the two of us.

The guy walking next to me was the one who wondered if Kenny was staying with Barbie. "So tell me, you came out here with that Barbie model? She as hot as she looks?"

"Hotter," I said. "The term sizzling have any connotations?"

At this point, Donner turned around and looked at him.

"Man," he said and just shook his head.

Thirty-one

Over a couple of beers, we reviewed the evening and tried to figure out what was going on and what I was supposed to do that would make Tubby happy and get him off my back.

"It just seems to me that if we keep an eye on Kenny, don't let him wind up with this Paulo character, that's all the guy wants," Goose said. We were seated at a corner table in the back of a little bar Goose went to from time to time.

"How does Tubby Gustafson, sitting back in St. Paul, even know Kenny exists? Right out of the starting gate, I don't get that," I said.

"Maybe he didn't know, maybe he just heard about my brother because of the Barbie photoshoot."

"But he knew about him before I even left to come out here. He knew about him before The Palms ever saw Barbie and decided she was the one they had to have."

"Oh, yeah."

"You said there was a high stakes tournament tomorrow night."

"Yeah, blackjack."

"Maybe Tubby's planning something for that?"

"Well, he might be, except that it's completely secure. The thing is televised on a couple of different cable channels. They'll have cops all over, along with their security team. Oh, and, by the way, Kenny isn't involved in it."

"Then why were those jerks outside the Barbie suite tonight? And why did they drop us off in the middle of nowhere and make us walk home? God, we could have gotten lost and died from heatstroke or something. Why were they trying to cuddle up to Kenny in the first place?"

"Well, with the dropping us off in the middle of nowhere, I figure they were giving us a warning," Goose said and drained his glass. "But it's like we're so dumb we don't even know what they were warning us about."

That seemed to pretty much sum up the situation.

"What are the chances of someone breaking into the Barbie suite tonight?" I asked.

"Just about zero. They're going to have someone in the hallway outside the suite until tomorrow morning when the makeup crew and the photographers start to arrive. Sounds like they were planning to do that anyway, just a lucky break we happened to show up before they had anyone posted. Like they said, today was a much bigger success than they expected, and the crowds just caught them off guard."

"Now they've got the name of that Paulo Caputo guy, and my boss sent them that photo online, so they'll be keeping an eye out for him."

"God, they had that huge crowd today, and they didn't even advertise it, just leaked the info to some news station, and all these Barbie wackos showed up. I wonder what tomorrow will be like?"

Goose shook his head, "Kenny. Man, the guy just always falls into a bed of roses, you know? Hey, sorry about Barbie dumping you."

I shrugged. "If I look back, I should have seen it coming. You know how they get. It's all fun and games, and then one day they wake up, see a friend pushing a baby stroller or something, and they're suddenly looking for a commitment from you, and they want a plan for the next twenty years."

"She did that, wanted a plan?"

"No, but I've been there before, and I could feel it coming. Hey, as long as they're going to have security up there, I think I'm gonna take off. I gotta grab Morton from the Groom Room."

"You see that little blonde down there?"

"Ramona, yeah, nice kid."

"She's not a kid, Dev. I know she looks like she's in high school, but she's close to thirty. Plays the teen angle on everyone, maybe you should check her out."

"Actually, I'm kind of liking things calm and quiet right now. I'll be over here in the morning, any chance you can make it?"

"Let me check with work, they're pretty good about that stuff as long as you give them a heads up, and after tonight's nonsense, if I come over here, The Palms will owe us. Always nice to have a favor out there you can call in."

We finished our beers, and I grabbed a taxi back to the Bellagio. I got down to the Groom Room just before they locked up. A guy was behind the counter.

"You here for Morton?" he said as I walked in.

"Yeah." I guess I sounded surprised.

"He's been our only guest today. It was so quiet, I hope you don't mind, but I ran him for about an hour and a half chasing tennis balls."

"No, that's great, I've been busy and haven't had a chance to pay much attention to him."

"Well, he's gonna sleep tonight."

"Thanks, I appreciate it."

He brought Morton out a moment later. His tail fired up as soon as he saw me. "Yeah, good to see you, too, buddy. Come on, let's go up to the room and take it easy."

We spent the night stretched out in bed, watching a movie, I can't even recall what we were watching. It was so interesting we both fell asleep halfway through it.

Thirty-two

I had Morton out on a walk the following morning before seven. It was already a cool eighty-eight degrees and climbing. We must have done three miles up and down the strip in about forty-five minutes, and it felt great. I grabbed a shower, dropped Morton off in the Groom Room with Ramona, and called Goose. I ended up leaving a message. I grabbed a taxi and headed over to The Palms. The driver dropped me off two blocks away to avoid the line of traffic waiting to get into The Palms, and I walked the rest of the way. Three cops were in the street, attempting to direct cars, none of which seemed particularly interested in taking direction.

More of the same, the Barbie crowd. A lot of pink t-shirts, dresses, and people laughing. I was going to keep my eyes peeled for Paulo Caputo, but it quickly became obvious that was a futile undertaking. Once I got inside The Palms, I headed for the security office Donner and his group had brought us to the night before.

"Hi, can I help you?" a guy said from behind a receptionist counter. He looked to be maybe mid-fifties, and if I had to guess, I'd say he was a retired cop. He was certainly friendly, but there was something there like he was doing a very quick in-depth estimate of me.

"Yeah, I was down here last night with Mr. Donner and some others. Myself and another guy stopped two guys with a gun from going into the Barbie suite up on the twenty-sixth…"

"Are you Arthur Gander from the Bellagio?"

"No, my name is Devlin Haskell, I…"

"You're the P.I. from the midwest, right?"

"Yeah."

"Minneapolis?"

"No, St. Paul."

My answer brought a smile to his face. "Yeah, people from St. Paul always make a point of stating they're not from Minneapolis, and Minneapolis folks always make the point they're not from St. Paul. So what can I do for you? Oh, I'm Everett Jackson, by the way," he said and extended his hand.

"Nice to meet you, please, call me Dev. You from Minnesota?"

"No, Chicago. I like winning teams," he smiled.

"My friend from the Bellagio was going to try and be over here today. He had a photo of a guy named Paulo Caputo sent over yesterday. That's the guy we chased last night, the one who fired the shot in the stairway."

Jackson nodded. "Yeah, every one of our guys has his image on their cell phones, along with a copy that was printed off last night. We've all seen the tape of him and some big dumb bastard running down the stairs. It looks like someone opened the door for them on twenty and, well, you know the rest."

"Did you get any images off your tape?"

"Yeah, but they're worthless. By the time we blow them up to a size where they might help with identification, they're so grainy they do anything *but* help. We did hear from the Bellagio, that's why I thought you might be Gander. He's supposed to be coming over and…"

"Hey, Dev," Goose called as he came through the door. He nodded at Jackson and said, "I'm Arthur Gander. Everyone calls me Goose. Sorry I'm late, I got held up in all the traffic out there. Looks like it's going to be another crazy day."

"Nice to meet you," Jackson said, shaking hands with Goose. "We got the blackjack tournament tonight, that's a level of pure insanity all on its own. Then some clever nitwit up in marketing decided it would be a good idea to schedule this Barbie nonsense at the exact same time and, well, you just can't make it up. Why bother to check with the folks who are supposed to make sure nothing bad happens?"

"If I had to size it up, I'd say the crowd this morning looks a lot larger than yesterday's," Goose said.

"That's 'cause last night all the stations covered yesterday's Barbie orgy on the six and ten o'clock newscasts, spreading the word there would be more of the same today. I don't know if we paid for that publicity, but it would have been nice to get a heads up. Everyone's been called in for double shifts. I got a lot of unhappy campers up there trying to keep things a semblance of sane."

"How can we help?" I asked.

"I love ya, but just stay the hell out of our way, and we'll all get along fine. Barbie was supposed to knock off around four, but I just got an email that said she's going to be making a special appearance at eight tonight to kick off the blackjack semifinals. The term clusterfuck have any connotations for you guys?"

Goose and I laughed and nodded, Jackson was right. It seemed like the left hand didn't know what the right was doing. Goose said, "You know what might help? If we could get a passkey just so we could ride the elevators. I can't do much on the Barbie group when they're out on the casino floor, but I know they're going to be doing some of that photoshoot in the Barbie suite, and if we could get up there and just stay in the hallway, it could free up another guy or two for you."

Jackson seemed to think about that for a half-second, then said, "Damn good idea, duck."

"It's Goose," Goose said.

"Yeah, sure, whatever. Tell you what, give me a couple of minutes, I'll get you those cards and some phones. As long as you're gonna be up there, you might as well be able to get in touch with us. Hang on while I get it lined up.

Thirty-three

Goose and I were up on the Casino floor with white earbuds in our ears and electronic master keys for the elevator and door locks in our pockets. More pink velvet ropes cordoned off an area around one of the roulette wheels. A pink sign with the blue Barbie logo sat on an easel next to the roulette table announcing that Barbie and Ken would be down at one fifteen to try their luck at roulette. That was more than three hours from now, and there were already hundreds of people waiting, most of them women in various shades of pink, and then the occasional bored-to-death-looking husband.

Goose and I attempted to scan the crowd and quickly found the effort a waste of time. "I'm thinking we head up to the twenty-sixth floor and see how the loving couple is doing," Goose said.

"Yeah, fine with me. But I think it might be a good idea if I just stay out in the hall. Barbie was stressed enough yesterday, and today is going to be even crazier. You can go in and check on your brother, but please, don't mention my name."

We flashed our master keys at the security guy stationed next to the bank of elevators. He gave us a questioning look when he saw the white earbuds but waved us through. We hopped on an elevator and shot up to the twenty-sixth floor.

"Little better than yesterday, ain't it?" Goose said as we stepped into the hallway.

"I'll say, nice job getting us lined up with these."

"I just hope we're totally bored today," Goose said as we headed down the hallway.

There was a two-wheeled dolly in the hallway next to the door to the Barbie suite. Two large black plastic containers were stacked on it. Three more containers were stacked one on top of the other next to the dolly.

"Photography stuff, I'm guessing," I said.

Goose popped the lid on one of the containers. It was crammed full of extension cords. "I'll check inside, you sure you don't want to come in?"

"Bad idea. Like I said, don't even mention my name."

"Yeah, but you're out here keeping her safe," Goose said, then saw the look on my face and said, "Okay, okay. Mum's the word, man. I'll be back in just a minute." He slipped his pass card in the electronic lock, the lock gave an audible click, and in he went. I kept an ear to the door for a long moment but didn't hear any screaming or swearing, so I figured things were going okay. Goose came back out about an hour later.

"What were you doing in there, Goose? Hey, is that frosting on your lip?" I asked, and he rubbed his upper lip, removing whatever it was.

"Sorry, man, they had a bunch of sweet rolls and shit. None of the women were eating them, so I figured the least I could do was…"

"You didn't think of me out here, the first line of defense?"

"If you want, I can go back in and get you one. They're really good."

"Never mind. Are they taking pictures in there?"

"Yeah, clicking away. Of course, Kenny's always had this thing with numbers, so he's giving everyone the picture count every thirty seconds. No one's told him to shut up so far. We'll see how long that lasts."

"Barbie in there?"

Goose nodded.

"Did she ask about me?"

"No, she didn't, and I followed your specific instructions and never even mentioned your name."

"Probably a good idea. What are they photographing?"

"Mostly, Barbie. They got her taking all sorts of poses next to the paintings and chairs, making the bed, standing next to—"

"Did Kenny spend the night there?"

"I don't know, and I didn't think it would be the best idea to ask."

"Probably wise," I said, although I really wanted to know. "What's she wearing?"

"When I left, a pink skirt with a white dog on it, the thing sticks out like this," Goose indicated by circling his hands around his waist.

"I think they call that a poodle skirt."

"Well, I lost track of how many outfits she had to change into. They got three racks full of all sorts of outfits."

"She must be loving it. Is Sugar in there?"

"Her dog, yeah. She and Kenny get in a picture every once in a while probably so they don't feel left out. That Diamond guy is in there, directing. That Camille woman is in there, too, some makeup folks standing at the ready with little brushes and tissues. Actually, as goofy as it sounds, it's quite the production. Tell you the truth, I sure as hell wouldn't want to do it."

"Anyone say anything about Caputo last night?"

"No. I'm not even sure they know about it, and I wasn't going to bring it up. I'm thinking even Diamond probably doesn't know."

We stood in the hallway leaning against the wall for almost two more hours.

"You feel like getting something to eat?" Goose asked.

"I think one of us should probably stay up here. You go ahead and grab some lunch and just bring me something back."

"Okay, I should be back in about a half-hour, anything special you want?"

"No, whatever you get will be fine."

"Okay, set your watch, thirty minutes," he said and
hurried down the hallway.

Thirty-four

It was closer to an hour before he finally made it back, carrying what looked like a white bakery bag. "I was beginning to wonder if I should send out a search party."

"It's crazy down there. The casino is jammed with people waiting for Barbie's appearance. Every place with food had a line a mile long, I finally cut to the head of a line and pulled the 'security guy in a hurry' routine and got some something to eat. Hope you like soft shell tacos," he said, opening the bag. He handed me a taco then grabbed another for himself.

I was halfway through mine when three guys came walking down the hall. I recognized one of them from the security guys last night.

"What are you two bozo's doing up here?" Fortunately for us, he said it with a smile.

"Your man Jackson deputized us," Goose said and took another bite of his taco. "Umm, you guys been working down there on the casino floor?"

"Absolute insanity. They called everyone back in for a double shift. I'm going on about four hours' sleep, and we got that damn blackjack tournament tonight.

They're already playing the qualifying rounds now. Must be close to a thousand players, at a grand apiece just to enter, that's a million bucks, cash right there. A million here, a million there, gee after a while it starts to add up. I'll probably fall asleep standing up before the tournament is over tonight."

"You here to bring Barbie down to the roulette wheel?"

"Yeah, her appearance is scheduled for one-fifteen. We called up about forty-five minutes ago. We're going to haul them down in one of the freight elevators. Her fans got the hall around the elevators so crammed with chicks waving signs and Barbie dolls it's impossible to get anywhere. I'm talking grown women, here, not little girls."

"Lot of nice looking ladies," one of the other guys said and grinned.

"I just hope we can get 'em down there and then back up here as soon as possible, maybe that'll start clearing some of the crazies out of the casino."

"I thought they had her making an appearance to kick off the semi-finals in the blackjack tournament to-night," Goose said.

"Yeah, but that's a private appearance, you gotta buy a ticket to get into the hall. Those gals downstairs are having a good time, but I doubt most of them are willing to fork over a C-note to get in and watch black-jack. I'm not even sure they could buy a ticket even if they did, I think the things been sold out for at least a month. Well, if you'll excuse us, duty calls. Nice seeing you guys again."

"Soon as you go in the suite, we'll head downstairs," Goose said, then took another mouthful of taco and watched as they pushed the door open and entered. We finished our tacos on the elevator then stepped off on the first floor into a sea of pandemonium.

A loud cheer and screams started to come from the crowd then died off just as quickly once people realized it was only Goose and I. Women waved signs saying 'We love Barbie.' The crowd was a sea of pink; Barbie dresses, hats, hairbands, feathered boas. A number of fans waved Barbie dolls, and at least three women wore Barbie swimsuits, one was in a very small black and white bikini.

"Check that chick out," Goose said, staring as we passed her. "She must not have gotten the memo."

"Actually, that's the pattern from the original Barbie swimsuit."

"You, you actually know that? How in the hell— Oh, yeah, I forgot."

"If Kenny clicks into all the Barbie trivia out there, the way his mind works, she'll never let him go. I mean, take a look around," I said as we began to push our way through the crowd.

No one seemed to be interested in moving. They were all trying to look over, around, and past us to catch a glimpse of Barbie who was due to arrive at any moment. We got more than our share of dirty looks, a few colorful comments, and someone grabbed my butt. Eventually, we made it through the crowd, which was still attracting more and more fans.

Up ahead, security guys were working at trying to keep the main aisle clear and seemed to be failing. The area was lined with more pink velvet ropes and more fans dressed in a variety of pink ensembles.

"Looks like a Pepto Bismol shareholders meeting," Goose said as we headed toward the roulette table where Barbie was scheduled to appear. We got about halfway there and had to stop due to the crowd. I spotted Donner up ahead, trying to get the crowd to move back so normal folks could get past. He kept pushing his hands forward in an effort to get the crowd to move, only there was no room for them to move. We shouldered our way toward him.

"Donner," Goose called. "Having fun yet?"

He gave us a look that suggested he was not in a laughing mood. "This is just nuts, and you know the really great part? No one is spending any money. We've had to shut a number of games down because no one could get to the tables to play. All the paying customers, you know, the folks we make money from, they've all fled the scene and gone over to Caesar's, the Bellagio, or the Flamingo. We're stuck with these Barbie crazies."

"How can we help?"

"You could get me a fifth of Maker's Mark and a quiet corner," he said then shook his head. "Actually, they got her highness and company waiting back there on the freight elevator. If you could get to them, I'm sure they could use two more bodies to try and keep this mob away."

"Where do we go?"

"Go up to the main desk, take a right, and at the end of the desk, there's a steel double door. They give you master passes?"

Goose nodded.

"Go in and about halfway down the hall on the left are the freight elevators. They'll be waiting there. I'll tell them you're on the way."

"It'll take a couple of minutes," Goose said as three women ducked under the velvet rope and started to run toward the roulette table. One of the women fell and landed face-first on the floor. Her friends either didn't see her or ignored her, it was hard to say which. She half-sat up as the crowd of people flowed past. Her nose was bleeding and dripping blood onto her pink Barbie top.

"Oh, shit," Donner said and went to help her to her feet. A half-dozen other women ducked under the ropes and hurried across. Goose and I spread about four feet apart and stopped the next batch from running across the aisle.

"Oh, please, we just want to see her?" a woman pleaded.

"She's not even there, besides I think they might have moved her appearance to a different area because there's so many people," Goose said. Suddenly you could see the heads turn and begin spreading the word through the crowd.

Donner came back gently guiding the woman with the bloody nose, she was holding a cloth up against her nose, but I could still see some blood dripping onto her top. "I've got to escort this woman downstairs to the infirmary and get her checked out. Let me notify the group, tell 'em you two are heading their way," Donner said then spoke into a microphone attached to his shoulder.

"Yeah, Tommy, I'm sending two more back to you." He gave us a nod and indicated we should head for the lobby. "No, they're all I've got. It's nuts out here," he said, and then we were too far away to hear him speak.

Thirty-five

We actually made better time than I thought we would, although you could see where a number of gaming tables had been closed due to the crowds, and I was sure his assessment of the event actually costing the casino a lot of money was accurate. Goose slipped his card into the slot next to the steel double doors, there was an audible buzz, and we pushed through and hurried down the corridor.

If the casino was all lights and glitz, this behind the scenes area was strictly industrial. A polished concrete floor, walls on either side of the hall lined four feet high with a rubber or vinyl coating and overhead inset lights with a sprinkler system running the length of the corridor. Every thirty or forty feet, there was a door labeled with whatever was on the other side, offices, a bar, maintenance. The bank of freight elevators was halfway down the corridor, off to the left, just like Donner had said.

We rounded the corner and were greeted by Kenny, smiling and saying, "Hi, guys."

At the same time, Barbie looked at me and said, "Dev, what are you doing here?" She was attired in a tight-fitting, pink, halter-top gathered dress with iridescent sequins and rhinestones. The outfit would just barely cover her, maybe, as long as she didn't move. The top was strapless, wrapped around her neck, exposed a massive amount of cleavage, and barely held her attributes in. She wore matching pink stiletto heels. The actual heels themselves were a sparkly gold and a gold belt with a large gold buckle that looked like she'd just won the world boxing title hung loosely around her waist. Sugar squirmed in her arms. Kenny, by comparison, was in your basic khaki trousers and an untucked, blue, buttoned-down shirt.

Diamond, Camille, a couple of makeup people, and the three security guys made up the rest of the group.

"How is it out there?" the security guy we'd spoken with in the hall outside the Barbie suite asked. Goose just gave him a look, and the guy said, "Yeah, I was afraid of that."

"You Tommy?" Goose asked.

"Yeah." Then he gave a quick look around and said, "Okay, let's go. We're going to be cutting through the Social Club, the table we're using is set up just outside. I need everyone to stay close, it's really jammed out there," he said, then shot a quick look at Diamond, who seemed oblivious, and we all started down the corridor.

"Once we get out of the Social Club, the table is just to the right. We'll tighten it up around our two rock stars. If you guys can try and move folks aside so we can get through, that'll really help. They got a couple more guys already stationed at the table."

A minute later, he slowed in front of the door labeled Social Club. Below that was a sign that read 'No Deliveries After 4 PM.' He pushed the door, and we all filed in, walking through the kitchen area with cooks dressed in white minding sizzling pans and steaming pots. We moved out through swinging double doors into the dining and bar area, heads turned, and then the comments started the moment Barbie and Kenny appeared.

"Oh. My. God. It really looks like her. Let me get a picture," someone said, and suddenly a number of women from all over the room attacked with their cellphones. We kept moving toward the front entrance. We could see the crowd outside, although things appeared to be deceivingly under control.

"Let's hold up for a second," Tommy said and brought us to a halt. "Okay, tighten it up group. Let's stay really close together out there," he said as cellphone cameras continued to flash around us. Barbie attempted to tug at her hem, which just seemed to bring attention to everything that wasn't covered.

"Nice ass," someone seated at the bar said.

"Let's go," Tommy said and stepped toward the entrance.

One woman hurried over and turned with her phone mounted on a selfie-stick then said, "Wait just a minute, I need to get everyone in this shot. Can you two get out of the way?" she asked Diamond and a security guy.

They both ignored her and headed out the entrance into the main casino. We made it five or six feet before the screaming and cheers started. You could sense the mob catching on to where we were as they rushed in the general direction. A couple of stools were tipped over, someone in the crowd fell, and another half-dozen people went down falling over her. Goose and I were pushing people back as they swarmed toward us.

"I just want my picture with Barbie," a woman said as she and her friend tried to duck past me. I tried to be polite and said, "Sorry,"

"Asshole," she shouted as we moved past.

"Ken, Ken," a woman shouted from the crowd. "We have the same birthday."

There was a lot of, "Barbie," and, "Love you," calls shouted along with a number of high pitched whistles and screams. It was like being at a rock concert with teenagers.

We made it to the cordoned-off area where the roulette table was. The croupier, there were three of them, kept looking at the crowd surging back and forth like a giant human wave as people from behind attempted to push forward, and the folks in front tried to hold their positions. There were two uniformed police officers in the area, too, and I was awfully glad to see them. Two of Diamonds' photographers began taking pictures of Barbie and Kenny standing around the roulette table. They posed with stacks of chips, smiled, and chatted with the croupiers and posed next to the roulette wheel. All the while, cellphones held high in the air flashed across the crowd.

After probably fifteen minutes of posed photos, Diamond gave the word, and the croupier said, "Place your bets," then he spun the wheel one way and the ball the other. Barbie placed a stack of chips on a diamond-shaped area that was red and labeled as such, then looked at Kenny, smiled, and nodded. Kenny shrugged as the ball made two or three more spins around the wheel before it bounced a half-dozen times and finally settled into the twenty-nine black slot.

Barbie looked disappointed. The crowd booed and hissed as the croupier raked in her stack of chips. He said something to Barbie, but I couldn't make out what it was.

A woman standing nearby said, "Aren't they going to let her win? It's Barbie for Christ's sake."

The croupier sent the wheel spinning one way and the ball going round in the opposite direction again. "Place your bet, Barbie."

This time she set a stack of chips dead center on the number nine and another stack on the same red diamond then looked at Kenny for some kind of moral support. I guessed she chose nine because the ninth of March was her birthday. It didn't really matter. The ball spun around a few more times, bounced back and forth, then settled into black twenty-two.

Barbie stomped her foot and angrily shook her head back and forth like a six-year-old having a tantrum. The crowd booed, this time a little louder, and the croupier nervously looked from the crowd to one of the cops as he raked in both of her stacks of chips.

Barbie said something to Kenny. Whatever it was, he nodded and pointed to the board just as the croupier spun the wheel and the ball and said, "Place your bets."

Barbie placed a smaller stack of chips, she only had about ten left, on the black twenty, then looked at Kenny. Kenny leaned forward and moved the small stack so that it was perfectly centered between four numbers, seventeen, eighteen, twenty, and twenty-one. The ball bounced a few times then settled into the seventeen slot.

"Barbie is a winner," the croupier shouted and smiled. He looked relieved as he glanced around at the crowd. Everyone cheered, cameras flashed, and then Diamond had the two professional photographers take about a hundred pictures of Barbie raking in her winning chips. This went on for another twenty minutes, Barbie placing a bet, usually losing, then placing one with Kenny's input and winning. Kenny never did bet on a specific number, but rather on the even, odd, red, black or the intersection of four numbers. He won more times than he lost, accumulated a larger pile of chips than Barbie had, and I wondered why he didn't do this for a living.

After a good forty-five minutes, the security team got ready to move. Barbie was handed a tray with her winnings along with Kenny's winnings conveniently filling the tray, which she now held up in the air for the crowd to see. The assembled multitude cheered and whistled. Then, with the help of the two police officers, we made our way back toward the social club.

Goose and I were in front clearing the way, maybe it was because the cops were with us, but it seemed a lot easier going than when we had arrived. The crowd was still there, but they didn't seem to be pushing and shoving as much to get closer. They just stood there and watched. There were still all sorts of cellphone cameras flashing, but the crowd was definitely more in control.

We had to walk up three steps to enter the Social Club area, and as we climbed to the top, I glanced out across the crowd and there, off to the side, I saw him. Paulo Caputo. He was wearing a blue and pink jersey with 'Barbie' scrolled across the front and a pink Barbie baseball cap. He had a two-day growth of beard on his face that gave me pause for a moment, but it was definitely him.

"Goose, Paulo Caputo," I said as we entered the relative sanity of the Social Club. "See him back there by the blackjack tables. He's wearing that pink baseball cap. Right next to that woman with the headband that has two pink stars standing up and bouncing back and forth."

Goose looked in the general direction for a long moment, then said, "Yeah, the guy in that pink jersey? Took me a minute with the beard thing going on. What do you want to do?"

"Not much we can do. He'd see us coming a mile away and disappear. Maybe give Jackson a call, tell him we spotted Caputo, give the description with the hat and the jersey. Can't be that many guys here wearing a Barbie jersey."

Goose nodded, and we headed through the kitchen to the rear corridor. Once we were back near the freight elevators, everyone seemed to dial down a bit, and Goose radioed Jackson with an update on Caputo.

"Thanks for helping out guys," Tommy said.

"We saw Paulo Caputo out there, just sent the description to Jackson.' Goose said to Tommy as my phone suddenly buzzed in my pocket.

I pulled my cell out, saw it was a message from Jackson, and clicked on it. The message had the same picture of Caputo from yesterday, but Jackson had added a note with the update regarding his beard, the Barbie jersey, and baseball cap. "That was fast," I said.

"Everyone's wired with all this going on and the tournament tonight. At least this was the last appearance of little Miss Hottie until tonight, and that'll be private," Tommy said. "Hopefully things will empty out between now and then and get back to a semblance of normal. You guy's heading back to the suite?"

"Hadn't given it much thought to tell you the truth."

"They were supposed to bring a bunch of sandwiches and soft drinks up there while Barbie was playing roulette. Come on and join us. I can't attest to how good it'll be, but the price is right. Besides, you guys earned it. We were short-handed, and you really helped out."

With that, the freight elevator arrived, and we all got on and rode up to the twenty-sixth floor. We hurried down the hallway, although with no one around, we really didn't need to.

Kenny dropped back a little and said to Goose, "I think they took seven-hundred-and-thirty-seven pictures, but I can't be sure because it was so hard to hear with everyone screaming."

Thirty-six

We all wandered into the Barbie suite. Just about everyone made a B-line for the trays of sandwiches and the cans of soda pop except Barbie, who excused herself and headed into the bedroom. She was back in just a couple of minutes without the world's shortest pink dress, now wearing a bulky pink Barbie jersey just like Caputo had been wearing and pink sweatpants with a white stripe down the leg. She attacked the sandwich tray, stacked two onto a plate, added a brownie and a giant cookie, grabbed a can of soda pop, and wiggled her way onto the couch wedged between Kenny and Camille. Camille had to slide over a good foot to make room for Barbie, who then proceeded to turn her back toward Camille and cut Kenny off from everyone but herself.

I watched the antics and shook my head.

"You working the blackjack tournament tonight?" Goose asked Tommy.

"Yeah, they got everyone in pulling a double shift today. I'm already dragging, and we got at least another eight hours to go. Thankfully this stuff is over. I think from here on in they're photographing Barbie up here and holding off on the casino appearances. I guess she's got some TV interview tomorrow morning."

"TV interview?" I said.

"Yeah, one of those noon news shows. No real news, it'll be some chef with a recipe, something about whatever bands are here in concert and Barbie. It'll run on our in-house station and online when you click on the casino site. But that'll all be private so nothing like today or yesterday. You gotta give her credit, she sure as hell has a following."

"It's nuts is what it is," Goose said."

"Tell that to my wife. She was supposed to be down here with a couple of girlfriends if they could lineup sitters."

Kenny got up from the couch, looking a little uncomfortable, and walked over to us. He stared at the floor when he spoke. "Umm, Dev, ahh, sorry, but Barbie was wondering when you were going to leave."

Goose's eyes flared, and he said, "Kenny, tell her to get . . ."

"Relax, Goose. I'm about ready to head out, anyway. See if I can find Caputo or what he might be up to." I turned to Tommy. "They're not making any appearances until tonight?"

"Right, the next thing on the schedule is nine o'clock tonight when they kick off the semifinals in the blackjack tournament. That'll be in the private ballroom on the second floor. Little different crowd than this afternoon, the appearance will be a lot more low key and probably only last about four or five minutes. You guys going to be there?”

“I'd like to be,” I said.

“I got nothing else going,” Goose said. “I'll at least check it out.”

“I'll let Jackson know, make sure you can get in.”

“Kenny,” I said. “I'll see you later on, you go back and tell Barbie you kicked me out, told me to leave. I'm going to hurry out of the room, so you make it look like you threw me out.”

“I feel bad, Dev. I don't want you to leave.”

“Are we still pals?”

Kenny remained staring at the floor and nodded. “You know we are, Dev. You, me, and Goose.”

“Okay, good. You go enjoy yourself and put a smile on, pal,” I said and patted him on the shoulder.

“I'm about finished, I'll go with you,” Goose said.

“I should head out too, gotta walk through the ballroom, and check it out before tonight,” Tommy said.

We called our goodbye's to Diamond, Camille, and the photographers. I said goodbye to Barbie, but she kept her back to me, pretended she didn't hear, and focused on Kenny.

Out in the hallway, Tommy said, “What'd you do to her?”

“Nothing, it just came on as soon as Diamond made her the offer for the photoshoot she got this attitude that I was beneath her.”

“Could be a fun place to be.”

"It's no big deal. Hey, I guess we'll see you to-night."

"I'll just be glad when this is over, and we can get back to normal, whatever passes for normal in this town," Tommy said.

We took the elevator down, Tommy got off on the second floor, and waved goodbye. Goose, and I got off on the first floor and headed for the bar. There was still a preponderance of women attired in pink, but nothing like it had been just thirty minutes before. A group of maintenance guys were loading up the stands and the pink velvet ropes onto four carts. Two other guys were picking up the remnants of signs, the head from a Barbie doll, and just the general trash left in the wake of the mob.

"I'll buy the first round, two beers," Goose said as we climbed onto the barstools. Other than a couple at the far end of the bar, we were the only ones in the place.

"Amazing what a difference thirty minutes makes," Goose said as he tossed a twenty across the bar once the bartender placed our beers in front of us. She peeled a dollar bill from a wad in her pocket and placed it back on the bar. Goose just looked at it and shook his head. "Nine-fifty a beer, sometimes I hate this town."

"I'm thinking about Caputo."

"Yeah, you coming up with anything?" Goose said, then took a sip and nodded like the beer was maybe bet-ter than he had expected.

"The quarter-finals on this blackjack tournament that has to be it."

"You thinking he's going to rob the place? It'll be teaming with cops."

"No. I'm thinking Barbie figures into it somehow."

"Barbie? You heard Tommy. She's going to be there for four or five minutes tops. And by the way, if you know anything about the guys in this tournament, that's four or five minutes she'll just be in the way. They don't care who the hell she is or thinks she is. They don't give a rat's ass how sexy she looks or what she's wearing. They wouldn't even care if she wasn't wearing a stitch. They just want to get going with the cards. I'm telling you, she'll be in the damn way."

"But that's got to be it, there's nothing else."

"Maybe your pal Tubby was wrong. Maybe he made a mistake."

"It's not like him to do that. He's always been Mr. Inside information. I mean, if it wasn't for him, we wouldn't even know about Paulo Caputo and those other knuckleheads. I'm still wondering why they were trying to snuggle up to Kenny. That was the whole reason I came out here in the first place."

"I'm wondering if they didn't think Kenny had something to do with the tournament, something with the cards or card counting or something. They just guessed wrong and missed the boat. Other than working in the same building, he's not involved. Hey, your turn to buy,"

Goose said and drained his glass. I'd yet to touch my beer.

Thirty-seven

We finished our beers. Goose went home to take a nap, promising he'd be back before seven. I strolled down to the lower level and wandered into the security office. I found Jackson at the front desk behind mounds of paper and files.

He looked up as I walked in the door. "Hey. You'd think in the digital age we could find a faster way than this," he indicated the stacks of files. "God, I tell you. So, you survived the great Barbie event?"

"The roulette photoshoot?"

"Yeah, that brain-fart. All my guys are running on fumes at this point. If they could have put that nonsense off for just twenty-four hours, it would have really helped, but I guess the powers that be know better."

"You have some good professional people on your staff. It was a pleasure to work with them."

"Yeah, all in all, they're pretty good. Thanks for the update on Caputo, by the way. I sent it out as soon as I got it."

"Yeah, I noticed. That's what I wanted to ask you about. I'm still not getting it, Caputo. Obviously, he's not the first questionable guy you've had here and certainly not the worst."

"No, matter of fact, we had Charlie Sheen just last week."

"There you go. I just can't figure out what Caputo wants. Barbie? That doesn't make much sense. Your blackjack tournament? Security's going to be so tight some of the players may not make it in. But, there he is this afternoon watching Barbie play roulette."

"Maybe the guy is just crazy enough to be fixated on her."

"Barbie? No, I got word about him being out here before he knew anything about her before your marketing folks knew she even existed. Besides, if he was truly fixated on her, wouldn't he be up toward the front and try and touch her, or call to her or kiss her or something? I just happened to catch sight of him lingering back in the shadows for all practical purposes."

"Well, please don't take this the wrong way, but he's not our problem. Frankly, we'll keep a lookout for him, keep an eye on him if we do see him, but as long as he behaves himself, there's really not too much we can do."

I drummed my fingers on the desktop thinking. Then finally said, "I wish I could disagree with you."

I went upstairs and strolled around the casino floor. Looking around, you'd never guess pandemonium ruled here just a little more than two hours ago. The place seemed reasonably quiet for a casino in the late after-noon. A number of the tables that had been shut down were open again, and people were playing and enjoying themselves. I had to look to find anything pink, and when I did see it, it was a businessman walking past in a navy-blue blazer and grey slacks with a pink shirt. He proba-bly didn't have a clue who Barbie was. No sign of Paulo Caputo or any of his pals. I decided to head back up to the twenty-sixth floor and post myself outside the Barbie suite.

Boring doesn't do it justice. The hallway was empty. I stood outside the room for almost two hours and never saw or heard a sign of life. The elevator never even stopped on the floor. The two-wheeled dolly and the black plastic boxes that had been stacked outside the suite were long gone. I lost count of the number of times I put my ear to the door to see if I could hear something but never heard a thing.

My own paranoia started to take hold of me, and I had to constantly remind myself not to knock on the door. If Barbie was in there about the nicest thing she'd do would be to give me another blue plastic bag and tell me to take Sugar for a walk. Of course, she'd immedi-ately think I was groveling to get back in her good graces. Maybe get a goodbye quickie before I hopped on the plane tomorrow, and then that would just give her the pleasure of telling me 'no way' and 'was I sure I didn't want to take Sugar for a walk?'.

The only action I got was after a couple of hours when Goose sent me a text message saying he'd be down in a half-hour and wondering where we should meet. I texted him back saying I was outside the suite. He didn't reply.

He showed up about forty minutes later looking freshly showered and shaved, wearing a clean white shirt, pressed jeans, a grey blazer, and black cowboy boots.

"You going to be with me tonight, or you got a hot date?"

He shrugged and said, "These tournaments are pretty big things, a lot of high rollers. I just thought it might be nice to show up not looking like shit."

"You're suggesting I do?"

"I'm suggesting it's already been a long day, at least I had the good sense to grab a nap and make myself presentable. Anything from inside?"

"No, in fact, I'm not sure anyone is even in there. I listened at the door once or twice, but couldn't hear anything. I figured if they were taking a nap or something else . . . it maybe wouldn't be the best idea to disturb them."

"You have anything to eat?"

"I had one of those sandwiches after the roulette wheel shoot."

"It's gonna be a long night, why not go downstairs and get something in you. I'll stay up here. I'm sure they'll be getting a heads up call about an hour before, probably want to do Barbie's makeup and hair. I'll knock on the door in a bit. You go take it easy for forty-five minutes."

"You sure?"

"Get out of here, Dev. I think I can figure out how to lean against the wall for the better part of an hour."

Thirty-eight

I knew Goose was right, and I could feel myself beginning to dial down by the time I stepped onto the elevator. I grabbed a couple slices of pizza and a Coke at a little 'food on the go' counter, then just sat and watched people wander past. I lingered over the Coke for another ten minutes, then checked my cellphone for the time and headed back to the elevators. There was an hour to go before Barbie would make her appearance at the tournament, so the makeup folks would probably be up there getting her ready.

The twenty-sixth floor seemed just as quiet as when I'd left, and I figured Goose would be bored silly. I didn't see him in the hall, but then again, he did say he was going to knock on the door, so maybe they let him in, and he was talking with Kenny while Barbie got ready. I was halfway down the hallway when a voice called from behind.

"Hassle?"

I turned around and saw Diamond coming toward me with the makeup woman and the woman who had been doing Barbie's hair. I waited until they joined me.

"How's it going?" I asked as they approached.

Diamond puffed his cheeks, then blew them out. "Been a long day. Thankfully, this is the last appearance for today. I think we'll all be ready for a little R & R after this." The two women nodded, and we headed down the hall.

"Hopefully, you've had a quiet afternoon?"

"Quiet doesn't do it justice. Boring is more like it."

"Sometimes boring can be good," Diamond said.

As we drew closer to the suite, I noticed something lying in the hall. At first, I thought it might be something one of the photographers left behind, then immediately remembered the area was clear when I'd left Goose here. At the same moment, I recognized Goose's cowboy boot and picked up speed.

"How can some idiot lose one cowboy boot, at what point wouldn't you notice?" Diamond asked as I picked up the boot, then knocked on the door.

"You might want to knock a little harder. I didn't get a response when I sent them a text saying we were on our way, figured they were still sleeping."

I pounded on the door a couple of times, but there was no response.

"Oh, God, if they've gone off gambling or are out and forgot our appearance, I'll—"

I slipped my passkey into the slot, heard the lock click, and hurried inside. Goose was about fifteen feet away, lying on the floor and wrapped in fluorescent green duct tape. He had two black eyes, a swollen nose, and a fat lip. Blood was splattered across his white shirt, and the left shoulder on his blazer was torn.

"Goose, Goose, you okay?" I asked as I rolled him over.

Diamond hurried past me to Barbie, who was seated on the couch wrapped in the same green duct tape, wearing just a bra and a thong. A piece of tape had been placed over her mouth.

"Careful, Trudy, careful," Diamond said to the makeup woman. "We don't want to damage her skin." She ignored him and tore the tape off from Barbie's mouth. It sounded like a piece of cloth ripping.

"Ouch, God, are you crazy? Get this off of me, get it off me, get it off me!" Barbie yelled and turned to indicate her wrists taped behind her back.

I was calling 911, telling them to send an ambulance to the Barbie suite. Once I was sure that was accomplished, I called Jackson.

"Haskell, relax, I've got two fellows heading up there right now. They'll—"

"Someone got in here, beat the shit out of Goose. I don't know what they did to Barbie. They had her wrapped up in tape and—"

"What? If this is your idea of a joke, I'll—"

"I just got off the line with 911. They're sending an ambulance. Cops are on the way. They beat up Goose, damn it, they kicked the shit out of him."

"I'm on my way, stay there. We're coming."

It seemed to take forever, but I'm sure it was just a couple of minutes. I actually heard them running down the hall, and then the lock clicked, and the door opened. The security guy, Tommy, and another guy, who looked familiar but I hadn't officially met, hurried in. I'd gotten the tape off of Goose's wrists and ankles, and rolled him onto his back and set a pillow under his head. He was coming around, but he was still out of it. Someone had really pounded him. I noticed his right hand was purple and swollen, which suggested he'd maybe gotten at least one good shot in.

At this point, Barbie had her arms wrapped tightly across her chest, rocking back and forth, crying inconsolably. Diamond kept asking her what happened and who did this, but other than screaming to get the tape off, she hadn't said anything coherent. Trudy, the makeup woman, had her arm wrapped around her, and the other woman, the hairdresser, had just gone into the bedroom and gotten a robe to put around her.

Jackson entered the room a moment later, looking flushed and breathing heavy. He must have run all the way. He was followed by a couple more guys. At this point, there really wasn't much we could do. Jackson got on his cell, called someone from the infirmary, explained the situation as best he could, and told them to hurry. Then he placed another call to someone on his staff, quickly told them as much as he knew, and to tighten things up in the auditorium where the tournament was about to be held. When he disconnected, he gave me a look that suggested, *'What the hell else could happen?'*

He checked with Diamond and attempted to talk with Barbie, but his effort proved fruitless. She wasn't crying openly, but she was still rocking back and forth, quietly sobbing, and Trudy, the makeup woman, now had both arms wrapped around her.

Jackson came over to me just as the nurse from the infirmary stepped into the room. She was wearing powder blue scrubs with a stethoscope hanging around her neck. She carried a medical kit that looked more like a briefcase. She didn't so much as blink when she saw Goose but just got right down on her knees, opened the medical kit, and started in on him.

"How long has he been like this?"

"I left him a little over an hour ago, so it happened sometime after that. I'm guessing, maybe a half-hour, forty-five minutes, tops. We found him, both of them, about ten or fifteen minutes ago."

She pulled a syringe from her kit, pulled a plastic cover off the needle and squirted the thing in the air, then stuck it into Goose's forearm."

"You called the paramedics?" she said without looking up.

"They're on their way, along with the police," Jackson said.

She was gently running both hands along Goose's neck, then going out across his shoulders. She checked his arms, looked at that swollen right hand for a moment, then unbuttoned Goose's shirt.

After a bit, she sat back on her heels and looked at Jackson for the first time. "Obviously an assault, not as bad as it looks. I've given him something to put him out. They'll want x-rays, of course. I'm pretty sure there's a concussion. His nose is broken, probably the left cheekbone. He was hit with something fairly large and hard."

I immediately thought of Caputo's pal with the shaved head.

Goose suddenly gave out a groan and moved his head from side to side.

"Hey, take it easy, pal. You're going to be okay. Paramedics are on the way. She just gave you a shot, so you're going to be feeling sleepy."

He groaned like he was trying to say something, but I couldn't make it out.

"I'll be right back, I want to check on Barbie," the nurse said, then quickly got to her feet and carried the medical kit over near Barbie.

Goose moved his hand up against my knee, he attempted to say something, but it was barely a whisper.

"Just relax, Goose, you're going to be okay, man. You'll get the next couple of days off," I said, trying to make a joke.

He groaned a couple more times, each time just a little louder. "K-K-K, Kenny. Algo. Kenny," he said in a harsh whisper, and then his hand flopped to the floor, and he lay still, breathing deeply.

"Must be that med kicking in," Jackson said. "What's it mean?"

"Well, with everything going on, I completely forgot about Kenny. Do you know? Was he in here?"

Jackson had a blank look on his face as he looked around. "I have no idea," he said, then got to his feet and quickly checked the bedroom and the bathrooms. He came out of the second bathroom, shaking his head with his hands palms-up, indicating nothing. There was a loud knocking on the door, and one of the security guys opened it. Two cops and three paramedics stepped in. The paramedics rolled a gurney up alongside Goose, one of them just stood there trying to take in the decor.

The nurse from the infirmary had been sitting on the coffee table, trying to talk to Barbie. She got to her feet and came over, said something medical to one of the paramedics, and knelt down next to Goose.

"You find Kenny?" I asked, hoping I'd misread Jackson's body language.

"No, no, he's not here. Must have gone to his office or to get something to eat," he said, then turned and started answering questions from the cops.

I didn't think Kenny would have left Barbie. Did that mean someone grabbed him? And if so, who and why? I was thinking Paulo Caputo and that shaved head thug. But what could they possibly want with Kenny?

I hurried out of the suite, then got on my cell and called the main desk down in security, hoping Jackson had someone there in his absence. The phone rang a number of times, then there were some clicks, and I was afraid it was going to disconnect when a voice suddenly came on and said, "Security."

I told him who I was, said Jackson told me to check Kenny's office, but I didn't know where it was.

"Let's see here, Gander, Kenneth. Here it is, he's actually on the 'C' level. Room five 'C,'" the guy said after clicking some keys on his computer.

"'C' level. I don't know where that is. How do I get there?"

"Same level as accounting and the vaults. Take the elevator to the lower level, go left once you get off the elevator, there's two elevators at the very end of the hall. The one on the right takes you to the 'C' level."

"Lower level and go left," I said.

"Yeah, you'll need a passkey to use the 'C' level elevator."

"Jackson gave me one yesterday to access rooms and the elevators, will that work?"

"It's one of the security passkeys?"

"Yeah, at least I think so."

"Then it should work on everything," he said.

My phone suddenly disconnected as I stepped onto the elevator and pressed the button for the lower level.

Thirty-nine

I got out on the lower level, took a left, and ran down to the far end of the hallway. There were two elevators with steel doors, just like the guy described. I pressed the button for the one on the right, the door opened immediately, and I rode it down to the 'C' level.

I stepped out of the elevator and then had to pass through a security door that opened into the hallway. Fortunately, my security pass worked, and I was heading down a hall lit by fluorescent lights. Every other light seemed to be blinking.

If the corridor earlier this afternoon that we took going to the Social Club was industrial, this was a couple of steps down. The floors, walls, and ceilings were all grey concrete. The doors were steel and windowless and seemed to house a number of different offices on either side of the hall. Each door was numbered but had no other identification. Sections one and two took up more than half the offices and were numbered accordingly; 1-1, 1-2, and so on. The even numbers were on the right-hand side of the corridor, and the odd numbers were on the left. 'Five C' was a good way down the hall, and beyond that was a barred gate that looked like it would have been in a bank. I remembered the guy on the phone said Kenny's office was on the same level as the casino vault.

My passkey worked on the door, and I stepped into an austere set of offices that looked more like the faculty offices for a chemical engineering department at some university. If the offices were occupied, I couldn't tell, and I really didn't want to waste the time it would take to explain to someone why I was there.

A black plastic nameplate, 'K. Gander', was affixed to the metal door. The lock on the door looked to be the same as the ones to all the rooms. I slipped my passkey in, immediately heard a click, and opened the door.

Kenny's office was institutional at best, more like a cell. A green metal desk that looked like a relic from the 50s was in a corner facing the wall. A brown, two-drawer file cabinet sat alongside the desk. There was a laptop in the middle of the desk on top of a six-inch-high stack of printouts. Two large screens with keyboards sitting in front of them sat on a credenza alongside the desk. Both screens were flashing all sorts of numbers. I'd need two strong aspirin if I looked at them for much longer, and it struck me as strange that they would be on since, at least to my knowledge, Kenny hadn't been in the office for the past twenty-four hours. A series of indecipherable notes lay scattered around the desk, none of which I could read.

I opened his laptop, turned it on, and waited. That was about as far as I got, at no surprise, the thing required a password. I lifted the laptop up just to see if he might be as dumb as me and had taped the password on the bottom. Apparently, he was a lot smarter.

I did another quick look around, then called Jackson on my cell.

"Jackson," he answered, half-yelling and sounding stressed after just the one-word response.

"It's Haskell. You find Kenny anywhere? I'm down in his office, but there's no sign of him."

"No, been busy dealing with things up here. Para-medics left with Gander a few minutes ago. Doesn't look like any damage beyond what our nurse found, at least at this stage. I've still got the police here. We're getting Barbie calmed down and beginning to get some general info. I gotta run, I'll call you if we learn anything."

"What about the tournament?"

"I've exerted my authority, it's still going to go on, the tournament, but Barbie won't be making an appear-ance. Can you believe it?" he said, then lowered his voice, and I had a picture of him stepping into another room before he continued. "That idiot Diamond won-dered if we could move her appearance back a half-hour so they'd have time to get her ready. Talk about having your head where the sun don't shine. I told him, 'No f'ing way.' In fact, the cops are talking to her now, but once they're finished, I'm going to insist she spends the night in the hospital for observation. Nothing good is go-ing to come of her spending the night in this suite. You learn anything?"

"Yeah, Kenny is apparently smarter than me and doesn't need to write his password on the bottom of his laptop."

"He wasn't down there?"

"No, the place is empty, a stack of spreadsheets on his desk. He mentioned something about spreadsheets and having to go over them. I want to say he was otherwise detained groveling in front of Barbie and hasn't been down here for at least twenty-four hours. There are two computers on flashing all sorts of numbers. Does that make sense to you?"

"Two computers? Those two large screens on the credenza?"

"Yeah," I said, surprised Jackson was familiar with Kenny's office.

"And what's on the screens?"

"On the screens? Just a bunch of numbers flashing every so often, some are green, some are orange. Doesn't make any sense to me."

"Fuck, it's the vault," Jackson said.

"The vault?"

"Algorithms for the vault. The kid's got this thing for numbers. He was running tests on our algorithm security programs for the vault. Those computers shouldn't be on. Damn it."

"You got cameras in the vault?" I asked.

"Yeah, let me check right now with the desk. Do me a favor and walk down that hallway just to make sure everything is kosher."

"On my way," I said, disconnected and hurried out of Kenny's office. The hallway was empty and quiet as a tomb. There was a coolness to the air, almost damp but not really. I hurried toward the barred vault door.

The vault door had a pushbutton device attached to it where you'd put in the code. The door was still locked, but I could see in and down a little hall to a room with a long glass table. All sorts of metal boxes were scattered across the table and stacked against the walls. It was maybe a little crazy but didn't seem out of sorts. Then I noticed what looked like a small bundle of cash lying on the floor. Maybe a pack of tens or twenties with a band around them.

I called Jackson. "You see anyone in there?"

"No, it appears to be completely empty," I said.

"Empty? There should be a team of three."

"I can see into a room with a big glass table…"

"Yeah, that's the counting room."

"There's all sorts of metal boxes stacked against the walls and piled up on the table."

"Like how many?" he asked. Then said, "They're on the floor?"

"Yeah, lots of 'em, and I can see a bundle of cash on the floor, you know, just bills with a band around it, tens, twenties, or maybe hundreds. I can't tell what denomination from here, but it's just lying on the floor like someone dropped it."

"And there's no one in there?"

"Not that I can see."

"Shit," Jackson said and hung up.

Forty

I could hear them pounding down the hallway before I could see them. Three guys dressed all in black like the ones who met Goose and I coming out of the stairwell the other day. Only these guys wore flak vests and were armed with what looked like AK-47's. The vests had velcro along the side. One of them hung at an odd angle on a guy, and I realized in his haste to move, he'd probably attached the Velcro strips incorrectly.

A blonde guy with a crew cut brushed me aside, took one look through the bars at the room with the glass table, and said, "I don't believe it."

The guy with the flak vest hanging oddly just said, "Oh, shit."

"How long you been here, man?" Crew cut asked.

"Just a minute, maybe two. I was in the 5-C office, called Jackson, and he told me to check this out. I thought it looked okay until I saw that cash on the floor."

"Cash?" Crew Cut said, then turned to look in the vault again. He quickly talked into a radio on his shoulder, then seemed to listen from the white ear-bud set in his ear.

"No, it's confirmed, empty boxes all over." He wiggled the barred vault door, checking to see if it was locked. "No, it appears secure, but I don't see anyone, and the boxes are stacked all over the room. There's even a wad of bills on the floor they must have dropped. What? Yeah, he's standing right next to me. Okay, we'll be here."

"I don't know how," he said, looking at me, "but someone managed to knock us off. Jackson's on his way down. Track down the hall," he said to the other two guys. "We'll stay here."

The other two left on the run heading back the way they came. Jackson arrived a few minutes later, looking red-faced, and really stressed. He brushed past and peered into the vault. "Jesus Christ, how in the hell . . ."

A foot suddenly appeared at the corner of the door, then it kind of hopped and a little more appeared, only this time you could see some bright fluorescent-green around an ankle. The same color as the duct tape that had been wrapped around Goose and Barbie. Another hop, and suddenly it became apparent it was someone duct-taped to a chair.

The guy was balding, looked to be about fifty, wearing dark trousers, a white shirt, and a gold vest. A length of tape was wrapped around his head and covered his mouth. Tape bound his legs and arms to the metal chair. He hopped around until he angled the chair facing us, then stared wide-eyed and half-screamed through the tape covering his mouth.

Jackson was on his radio, "Dennis, override the counting room vault. No, there isn't time. I don't care. Yes, full responsibility. We've got at least one in there."

A moment later, there was a loud snap. Jackson pushed the barred door open and hurried toward the wide-eyed guy in the chair. Crew Cut followed him in, and I brought up the rear.

"Mario," Jackson called as he hurried over to the guy in the chair. He leaned over him and pulled at the edge of the tape from behind the guy's head, slowly removing it from the side of his face until he came to the guy's mouth. "I'm afraid this is going to hurt," he said, and then, before the guy could respond in any way, he yanked the tape off.

Bits of lip and mustache came off along with the tape, and Mario let out a high pitched scream, then shouted, "Son of a bitch!" and gasped.

"Sorry," Jackson said, then left the length of tape dangling on the far side of his face. Spots of blood and bits of mustache were attached to the adhesive side of the tape. Jackson directed his attention to the duct tape binding Mario's wrists to the arm of the chair.

Crew Cut had stepped past me and was working on freeing a grey-haired guy from a chair. I stepped over and began to work the same effort on a middle-aged blonde woman who sat there bug-eyed. They were all dressed the same, just like the dealers upstairs, black trousers, white shirt, and a gold vest.

"Get their arms and legs free, and they'll be able to deal with that strip over their mouths better than we can," Crew Cut said.

Mario took a deep breath and said, "Oh, Jesus, am I glad to see you, Jackson. Son of a bitch, you didn't catch any of this on the cameras? There were three of them. We'd just gotten the evening boxes delivered, plus the fees from the blackjack tournament. Bastards knew exactly what they were doing. Had that kid with them, the one that works on the numbers."

"Kenny Gander?" I said.

"Yeah, that's the one. We call him Rain Man," Mario replied as he carefully pulled the length of duct tape from the side of his face. "Looked like they'd roughed him up a little. They stuffed the cash in duffel bags and high-tailed it out of here. You had to have seen 'em."

I had both wrists free on the blonde woman and was on my knees working on her ankles. She was in the process of gingerly pulling the tape off from around her head. She made a hissing sound as she removed it from over her mouth, then suddenly shouted, "Bastards, I'll kill 'em, I swear to God, I'll kill all three of them!"

Jackson was on his radio, "Lyle, Lyle come in. Lyle? Lyle, where the hell are you? Shit," he said and took off running out of the vault.

Crew Cut looked at me and said, "Hold the fort down here. Mario, we're gonna need you three to stay put. It ain't safe out there right now. I want all of you to remain here. Okay?"

Mario nodded.

Crew Cut reached behind his back and handed me a small black pistol. The name 'RUGER' was etched just above the handgrip. "Keep everyone here, and don't let anyone in. This is a crime scene now. Mario, you're all going to be okay. I just want to clear the halls out here before we do anything else. I'll be back in five minutes, okay?"

Mario and the other guy nodded. The blonde woman half-groaned and said, "I gotta use the bathroom."

"Dorothy," Crew Cut said, "Can you hang on for five minutes? Please. We don't know where in the hell these guys are. Just hold on. Okay?"

"I can give you five minutes, but that's about all," she said and grimaced as Crew Cut hurried out of the vault.

"Look at this, look at this, can you believe it?" Mario said, looking around the room.

"You know the cops are going to want to ask you a lot of questions, what these guys said, what they looked like."

"Looked like?" the other guy said. "The bastards were wearing masks, for Christ's sake."

"You got some pens and paper in here?" I asked Mario.

"Yeah," he said, wondering what the hell I was talking about. "We always triple check our tallies."

"Maybe the three of you should sit down, start writing down anything and everything you can remember. What they said, how they walked, size, hair color, anything. Don't talk, just write down what you remember. That'll give the cops three distinct views. You may not know it, but each one of you is going to remember something unique that the other two didn't pick up on."

Mario shrugged as if to say, 'Might as well, we got nothing else to do.' Then he pulled open a drawer from the wall, took out three yellow legal tablets and some pens, and threw them on the table.

"I remember that they all smelled like pepperoni pizza or something," Dorothy said.

"We ain't saying anything, remember?" Mario replied.

"All right, all right, it's just that they smelled like pizza."

"Dorothy, come on, shut up."

They each grabbed a tablet and began writing. I checked out in the hallway, glanced at them writing, then went back to watching the hallway again. It seemed like we were in there forever before I heard something coming down the hallway. The three at the table heard it at about the same time and gave a worried look toward me. I waited until the figures came into view.

"Jackson and some cops," I said.

"Thank God," Dorothy said, standing up. "I really have to go."

Forty-one

They let Dorothy go to the bathroom, then separated all of us and began asking questions. Jackson was part of the group being questioned, not because he was suspect, but because he had information they needed to know.

They found Lyle, the guy Jackson had called, and then ran off to check on when he didn't answer. Unfortunately, they found him dead. Jackson had left him in charge of watching the security cameras for the stairwells and the lower levels. Someone, we're guessing the robbers, shot him at his desk, then took the time to damage the computer system attached to the cameras. Not that it couldn't be fixed, but that would most likely take hours, if not a day or two, and give the robbers more than enough time to casually leave town.

I told the detective interviewing me about Paulo Caputo, how he and his two friends dropped Goose and me off in the middle of nowhere. Just for safety's sake, I didn't mention anything about Tubby Gustafson. With everything going on, I certainly didn't need that kind of problem. The detective interviewing me casually wrote down Paulo's name and the address 20 Spur Cross Circle, then asked me how long I'd know Barbie Dahl, and was her name really Barbie?

"Barbie? Aren't you going to check that address out, send a swat team over there? Caputo and those guys are probably loading up that van and pickup truck right now and getting ready to blow town if they haven't done so already. I'm sure they're the ones responsible."

"And they're sleeping on the floor in a vacant house? In Henderson? Which, by the way, just happens to be out of our jurisdiction."

"But that's where they are!" I shouted.

"Please, sir, we're all here trying to work together. We'll contact the police in Henderson at some point, and they'll send someone over to check."

"Send someone over to check? I'm telling you these guys have been casing this joint, the casino, for the past week or so."

"And you've seen them."

"Yes, God, are you even listening? I already told you. We chased them away from the Barbie Suite. I spotted them in the crowd watching Barbie play roulette earlier this afternoon. I think they even followed Barbie and me over here from the Bellagio a couple of days back."

"Sounds like he's got a thing for your lady friend, Barbie. Can't say as I blame him, she's very attractive, in a certain way."

"Barbie? He doesn't care about Barbie. Can you put two and two together? He was after Kenny Gander."

He gave me a questioning look. "So you're saying this Caputo fellow is gay? I'm not seeing how that's really relative to this investigation, but I'll make a note of it." He smiled in a way that suggested I was the one without any brainpower.

"Is there anything else? It's pretty late, and I guess I'd like to get back to the Bellagio. I'm on a plane tomorrow at noon, and I still have to pack."

"Yeah, now, about your flight home. Maybe check with us in the morning. We'll see what develops overnight. There's a pretty good possibility we'll want you to remain another day or two. Just in case we have any questions."

"You can't just call me? I mean, I know it's a different area code, ten numbers and all, but I've given everyone my phone number. Someone could dial it for you."

He gave me a long look. "There really is no reason for that kind of attitude, Mr. Hassle. I'm just doing my job in what is clearly a very difficult situation."

I saw no point in correcting him on my name. It would only lengthen the interview, which, in my opinion, was going absolutely nowhere. "I agree, it is a very difficult situation, and I want to thank you for interviewing me and listening to my facts. If we're finished, I'd like to return to my Hotel. I feel a headache coming on."

"Let me see about some aspirin for you."

"Thanks, detective, but I think it would be best if I just went back to my room."

He nodded like this made sense, then said, "Take care of that headache, sir, and check with us in the morning."

"Thank you," I said, then got out of my chair and left the room.

Forty-two

I grabbed a taxi back to the Bellagio and hurried up to my room. With everything going on, I'd left Morton on his own for far too long. I could only hope he hadn't wrecked the place.

I slipped my key in the slot, then opened the door to the room. Morton was standing on the couch, looking back at me. He dropped what was left of the pillow in his mouth, hopped off the couch, and tried to hide.

The room looked like some drunken rock star had trashed it. A trail of white feathers led from the bedroom and was scattered all over the living room. The bag of dog food had been ripped open and spilled across the carpet, so as I headed for the bedroom, my feet kept crunching on nuggets of dog food. Another pillow had been ripped open, and it looked like it had snowed in the bedroom, feathers a couple of inches deep covered the bed and the carpet. The covers were off the bed and left in various corners of the room. The chair at the desk was tipped over. Two towels had been dragged out of the bathroom and chewed up. In a word, the place was destroyed.

The perfect end to an awful day and I only had myself to blame. I took a deep breath, then grabbed the leash, coaxed Morton out from behind a couch, and said, "Come on, let's go for a walk. We could both use it." That started his tail wagging, and he bounded up on the couch, suggesting he knew all was forgiven.

We headed out the door, rode the elevator down to the main floor, and walked out of the building. It was well after midnight, and there was a sparse crowd waiting for the fountain show in front of the hotel, unaware it was finished for the evening. Morton did his business behind the building, and like the responsible citizen I am, I cleaned up after him.

On our way through the lobby, I saw the Avis counter and a nice-looking lady sitting there with apparently nothing to do. Twenty minutes later, Morton and I were heading into Henderson. If the police didn't think it was important enough to check on Paulo Caputo, maybe we could prove them wrong.

I had to pull over three separate times to look at a map, but after a number of wrong turns, I eventually made it to Spur Cross Circle. I turned onto the street and slowly drove down the block. I could see the house up ahead, the three 'For Sale' signs next to one another in the front yards were still there. In the driveway, I could just make out the black van and the red pickup parked in front of the garage.

I pulled over to the side of the street and climbed out of the car. The moment I started to walk down the block,

Morton began barking. I kept walking for a few more steps, hoping he'd stop, but his barking only grew louder.

I hurried back to the car before neighbors started looking out their windows. I opened the rear door, grabbed his leash, and held him close to me as we started back down the street. We made a casual walk past the van and the pickup truck and saw nothing that suggested anyone was inside. But then again, how would you know with the power off? Morton whined a bit when we passed the house and kept trying to look over his shoulder as we headed down the street. I had to jerk the leash a number of times to get his attention. We walked to the end of the block and then turned around and made our way back toward the car.

As far as I could tell, no one was watching. The lights in just about every house were off, but then again, maybe they were all vacant.

We walked past again, and Morton began to whine. I pulled him close with the leash so that he was almost rubbing against my knee. He tugged and whined, but he followed. We walked past the driveway with the two ve-hicles parked up against the front of the garage. When we were almost at the property line, we hurried across the gravel that served as the front yard and over toward the side gate.

The wrought iron gate was half-open, and it squeaked slightly when I brushed against it. We made our way to the back corner of the house and waited for a moment. I didn't hear anything other than my heart pounding as I peeked cautiously around the rear corner of the house. There was nothing to see, although there was a small solar light dimly illuminating the far back corner of the brick wall. The place looked just as bleak and empty as the other day.

I pulled out the Ruger Crew Cut had given me from the back of my jeans, and we slowly moved forward. I could see that the sliding door stood wide open, which struck me as strange. We waited against the rear of the house for at least another ten minutes to see if someone would come back outside, but, thankfully, no one ever did.

I cautiously approached the sliding door. Morton began tugging more and more aggressively the closer we got. I pulled hard a few times but couldn't seem to get him under control. He planted his feet and wouldn't move forward. When I yanked on his leash, he suddenly began barking, and I quickly turned to run out of the backyard before Caputo or, worse, that big thug with the shaved head came out.

It was pointless to run, all three of them were right there staring at us.

Forty-three

I wouldn't have recognized the guy named Danny, with the scar across the tip of his nose, at least not at first. But that was because his nose was gone. He was the middle body. The three of them, Danny, Paulo Caputo, and the thug with the shaved head, were lying neatly on the bottom of the empty pool. The shaved-headed thug appeared to have been shot a number of times in the chest, and it looked like his left eye was swollen and black. I remembered Goose's right hand looked injured and wondered if he'd done it.

At first, Paulo Caputo seemed to be staring off to the side, but then I noticed the back of his head had been blown away, and his skull was just at an odd angle. A stream of blood ran from his right hand. Blood from all three bodies had run down an incline that, in better times, had formed the deep end of the pool. The blood eventually made its way down the drain. I stood and stared for a long while, then hurried into the house.

There was a pizza delivery box from a place called Angelina's Pizzeria, and I suddenly remembered Dorothy's comment about them smelling like pepperoni pizza. A half-dozen pieces of crust were all that remained in the box.

Out in the living room, three sleeping bags and three suitcases were lined up next to the front door, the same items I'd seen in the upstairs room the other day. I didn't feel like going upstairs and turned to head out through the kitchen. There in the corner were what looked like three empty duffel bags. I moved one of the bags with my foot, not wanting to touch it in case the crime scene people discovered some trace from me. Morton immediately took hold of the thing and shook it. Something fluttered off to the side when I bent down to pick it up. I realized it was a hundred dollar bill. I tucked the bill in my front pocket and hurried back out through the kitchen. We quickly passed the pool with Caputo and his two pals and made our way back out the side gate.

We were halfway across the gravel area when a pair of headlights flicked on down the street and headed toward us. I ran over alongside the black van and waited until the car had passed. Morton began whining again, so I yanked on his leash a couple of times, but he wouldn't stop.

Suddenly, there was a loud 'thunk' sound behind me, and I half-jumped. Then it happened again, and once more after that. It seemed to be coming from the inside the black van, and I glanced around, then knocked twice on the side. Two thunks sounded from inside the van, and Morton barked.

I pulled the Ruger back out, held it in my right hand, then cautiously slid the side door open with my left. Morton immediately jumped inside. I didn't see anything at first, and then, there in the dark, I could just make out a figure with the wrists and ankles wrapped in fluorescent green tape.

The figure wore khaki-colored slacks and a blue, button-down shirt. One of the knees on the slacks was torn and blood-stained. I didn't have to pull the pillowcase off his head to know it was Kenny.

"Kenny, it's Dev," I said as Morton hopped back and forth over him. I reached into the van, grabbed him by the duct tape around his ankles, then dragged him toward the door. I pulled his legs out the door, then helped him to sit up and took the pillowcase off his head.

His face was bruised, and his upper lip was swollen, but he looked a lot better than Goose did. "Mmm-mmm," was all he could say with the tape wrapped around his head.

"I'm going to pull the tape off from your mouth, Kenny, it's probably going to hurt a little."

He nodded, and I slowly began to pull the length of tape off. As I got closer to his mouth, he reached up with his taped wrists and just yanked the length of tape off.

The bruised lip started bleeding, and he spit blood on me when he said, "Oh, Dev, God, am I ever glad to see you. Where are those guys? Are they in that house?"

"Don't worry about them, Kenny, they're taken care of. Let's get you untied here, and we better call the police."

Once I undid his wrists, he said, "Dev, I can get my ankles, you call the police, so they get here before those guys come out. I don't want to have to deal with them. They weren't very nice."

"Don't worry, Kenny, they're not going to come out. I got them tied up inside."

"You sure?"

"Yeah, they can't hurt you anymore. Don't worry."

"They were all hitting and kicking Goose, and they were going to hit Barbie if I didn't help them. I didn't know what to do, Dev. I didn't know what to do. Do you think I'm going to be in trouble? What about Goose, is he okay? Is he hurt?"

"He's fine. He's in the hospital because they want to make sure he's okay. We'll go see him, but we have to talk to the police first."

"Is Barbie okay? I tried to save her, but there were too many of them and—"

"She's fine, Kenny, she's safe. They took her to the hospital to keep an eye on her for the night. She's going to be all right, and I think you did save her, along with Goose, too."

"I didn't know what else to do, Dev. I just wanted them to stop hurting people. I told them, but they just wouldn't listen to me."

"Kenny, you did the right thing. You saved Goose, and you saved Barbie. Now here, you hold on to Morton. He wants to protect you while I call the police."

Kenny wrapped his arms around Morton and sat there with his ankles still taped together while I dialed 911. Morton licked his face.

Forty-four

We sat in the open side door of the van waiting for the police to come. We didn't have to wait long. I think it was only a minute or maybe two before we heard the siren. A second squad car arrived no more than thirty seconds later. There were maybe a half-dozen police cars in the street in less than ten minutes. Most of them kept their flashing lights on. Small clusters of neighbors watched from front doors and driveways, although no one ventured toward the driveway where we remained.

Paramedics arrived and treated Kenny's swollen lip with some salve and gave him a bottle of sparkling water. He wanted Morton to stay next to him, so they let him remain sitting in the van. Kenny kept his arms wrapped around Morton as I told the paramedics about Goose and Barbie in the hospital overnight for observation and wondered if they could transport Kenny there.

"Probably took them to either Desert Springs or Valley, we can check. What are their names?"

"His brother's name is Arthur Gander. The woman's name is Barbie Dahl. That's spelled D-A-H-L."

"This the woman I saw on the television earlier this evening? She actually looks like that kid's doll, right?"

"Yeah, I guess she's not as fun as she looks," I said and then felt bad for saying it. "And this Kenny was, well, Ken. It all happened at The Palms."

"Yeah, right, God, The Palms, it seems like everything's happening there, ain't that something. Pat," he said, turning to the guy next to him. "Call in and see if you can find out which hospital they ended up in, and we'll get this guy there, so he's near his brother and Barbie."

"Thanks, guys, I really appreciate it."

"Anything to help Barbie and Ken, can't wait to tell my daughter tomorrow morning. She'll go crazy," he laughed.

I talked to a couple of detectives for another hour or two. I was so tired I didn't know what time it was when I returned the car to Avis. Morton and I stepped onto the elevator and headed up to the room. I pulled the drapes closed in the bedroom just as the sun was coming up. Then I flicked a switch next to the door that lit up a 'Do Not Disturb' sign out in the hall. I gave Morton a dirty look as I gathered the sheet and a blanket out of different corners of the bedroom, then crawled into bed.

Despite the mess Morton had made, it felt wonderful to climb into bed and finally be able to close my eyes. He hopped up onto the bed, circled around twice scattering, feathers before settling down next to me. He let out a big sigh, and a moment later started to snore.

Forty-five

My ringing cellphone woke me the following morning. Morton had stolen the only functional pillow left in the room. He raised his head as my cell rang and gave me a look that suggested, 'It's for you,' then shoved his head beneath the pillow. I stumbled out of bed, waded through the ankle-deep feathers toward my pants, and was able to grab my phone just as it stopped ringing. I turned it on, swiped the screen, and saw a missed call from Goose.

He answered on the second ring. "When are you coming to get me?"

"More importantly, how are you doing?"

"I'll survive, maybe look little rough around the edges, but I'm okay. Thanks for all you did, Dev."

"How's Kenny?"

"He's gonna be fine. The cops are in talking to him right now. They were with Barbie earlier this morning. I'm next, I have to talk with them before I can get discharged."

"Was it Caputo?"

"Yeah, him and those other two jackasses. Same ones who left us out in the middle of nowhere. They were wearing masks, but there's no doubt who in the hell it was. As far as I'm concerned, they got what they deserved."

"So you already talked to Kenny?"

"Yeah, he told me about you finding them. I don't know, man, it almost sounds like they were set up. Like someone let them take all the risks and then hit them once they thought they were home free. Not that it's any sweat off of me. I'm just glad you got him out of there, I got a feeling whatever they had planned for Kenny wasn't going to be in his best interest."

"From the looks of things where they were staying, I'd say they were ready to leave town. Suitcases by the door, sleeping bags sitting there. Someone sure as hell knew what they were up to and…"

"Hey, I gotta run, I got company coming in that I have to talk to. I'll call you when they're finished with me," he said and then hung up before I had a chance to ask him where he was.

I went back to bed and slept for maybe another hour. I got up, took a long shower, and then got dressed. I remembered I had a noon flight I was supposed to catch, but when I checked the time it had left a half-hour ago. I called The Palms and asked for Jackson but ended up leaving a message. I called the Vegas police department next and talked to a guy who took my contact information and told me they'd be in touch if they had any questions. He didn't seem to pick up on the fact that I was the guy who'd found Paulo Caputo and his two jerk pals, and I didn't volunteer the information.

I brought Morton down to the Groom Room. He was all excited before we even made it in the front door. When we stepped inside, Ramona was seated behind the front desk reading a book. She looked up and shouted, "Morton! What a surprise, I thought you were leaving today." Then she hurried around the desk and ran over to give him a big hug. He replied with a number of licks and a tail that wouldn't stop.

"Slight change in plans. Can I leave him with you for the day?"

"Are you kidding? I might not give him back."

I went up to the front desk and asked to speak with someone about my room.

"Is everything all right, Mr. Haskell?" the woman asked once she got my room number up on her computer screen.

"Actually," I said and proceeded to explain Morton being left alone for too long and the current state of the room. I did mention the situation at The Palms, maybe embellished a bit, suggesting I'd been in a gunfight in the vault, then chased Caputo and six guys over to the house in Henderson.

"My God, it's been on the news all morning. We've been talking about nothing else. You were involved in all that?"

"Yeah, well, me and one of your security guys."

"Which one?" she asked, wide-eyed. The women stationed on either side of her were suddenly ignoring their customers and focusing in on our conversation. That was okay because both their customers were doing the same thing. Listening to us.

"He's a pal of mine from Minnesota. We were in the army together. Arthur Gander."

She got a blank look on her face, and one of the women next to her said, "Goose?"

"Yeah, Goose, he's in the hospital. I'm going to get him this afternoon, once they release him."

"Was he shot?"

"No, just a little roughed up. He was in the Barbie Suite and . . ."

"Those guys went after Barbie?" one of the customers asked. "They didn't hurt her, did they?"

"No, no, she's okay. She was just in for observation overnight to make sure everything was all right."

"What's the world coming to?" one of the women said.

A small crowd was beginning to form, and I said to the woman I'd originally been talking to, "Anyway, my dog was left alone a little too long, and he ripped one of the pillows a little, there's a couple of feathers on the floor, and I just wanted to alert your housekeeping staff, it might take a minute or two longer when they're in that room.

"Oh, that's very kind of you. I'll let them know right away," she said, clicking her fingers across the keyboard.

"Thanks, I'll also have to book the room for one more night. Just in case the police have any more questions. You know."

She nodded like she did know. Like people being questioned by the police was just an everyday occurrence at the Bellagio. "Consider it done, Mr. Haskell. Is there anything else I can assist you with?"

"No, thank you. You've been very helpful."

Some guy in the small group that had gathered around said, "You know, one thing that wasn't clear on the news report I saw this morning…"

Fortunately, my phone rang. It was Goose. "Oh, sorry, I have to take this."

"Is it the cops?" the guy asked as I walked away.

"Goose, what's the word?"

"They're finished for now," he said. "But it looks like it's going to be a long, ongoing investigation."

I noticed the guy who wanted to ask me a question had followed me and was politely waiting just a few feet away. "Where are you now?"

"We're all at Valley"

"I'll grab a taxi and see you there. Any chance they'll let you out today?"

"They're cutting the release papers right now, same for Kenny."

"I'm on my way," I said, then hurried toward the door.

"Say, say, I just had a question," the guy called, but I pretended I didn't hear him and made my way to the taxi rank.

The guy working the taxi rank opened the rear door to a white taxi and asked, "Where to?"

"Valley Hospital," I said, climbing in, and then he yelled the exact same thing to the driver and slammed the door closed.

Forty-six

The ride took ten or fifteen minutes. I stared at the place as we came around the corner and turned into the front-drive. It looked like a miniature casino. Three-stories high with big red letters running across the roof that read 'Valley Hospital.' The letters looked like they'd probably light up at night. There was a big five-pointed star attached just above the letter 'V' in Valley. Below that on the overhang above the front door was a smaller version of the red 'Valley Hospital' with the star and then the address; 620 Shadow Lane. I thought the street name had a sinister ring to it, but then again, we were in Vegas. The taxi pulled up to the front door. I paid the driver and hurried inside.

There was an information desk on the far side of the lobby. A woman with permed, white hair who looked to be in her mid-seventies was handling the desk. She had a black name tag labeled 'Volunteer' pinned to her blouse, and she had focused in on me from a distance of about fifty feet then watched as I approached. "May I help you?"

"Yes, I'd like the room number of Mr. Gander."

"G-A-N-D-E-R?" she spelled the name out.

"That's correct."

"Oh, dear, it appears there are two of them."

"I'm looking for an Arthur, well, and a Kenny, too. If that's them, both numbers would be good."

She eyed me suspiciously. "Are you family?"

I lied and said, "Yes."

That brought a smile to her face, and she said, "Rooms three-twelve and three-fourteen. They're right next to one another." Then she pointed toward a hallway and said, "The elevators are on the right, just press the three once you get on and follow the sign on the wall when you step off on the third floor."

I said, "Thank you," and thought she must have been a school teacher in her working life.

I came to three-twelve first and popped my head in the room. Goose was fully dressed in the clothes he'd worn yesterday. He was lying on the bed, watching television and sipping something through a straw. He saw me almost immediately and clicked the flat screen off with the remote.

"About time, Jesus, I was afraid if I was here much longer, they were gonna haul me away for an enema or something. Let's get the hell out of here." His left eye was swollen shut. He had a hell of a fat lip. The right side of his face was black and blue. He had gauze wrapped around his head and covering his ear. His right hand was encased in some kind of wrap.

"You all set to go?"

"Yeah, believe me, I just want to get home. I gotta call the nurse first," he said, then reached over with his left hand and pressed a button. "They have to push me out in a wheelchair, their rules. Did you drive?"

"No, I took a taxi."

"There's usually a couple out there. We can just grab one."

"What about Kenny?"

"He's, ahh, going to head back with Barbie. You know, get her settled into a different suite and all."

"I meant was he okay."

"Kenny, yeah, fine, just a fat lip is all. Barbie's okay, too."

"Good," I said but didn't offer anything further.

A moment later, a nurse came into the room, pushing a wheelchair. "Someone ready to flee the scene?"

Goose raised his hand, "Yeah, me."

"You sure? We could set it up so you could stay the weekend," she said, then rolled the wheelchair alongside the bed.

"Thanks, but no thanks."

"You need a hand getting in there, Goose?" He was grimacing as he slid his legs off the bed and wiggled himself toward the edge until his feet were on the floor.

"Nah, I got this. Maybe pop your head into the room next door and let Kenny know I'm taking off. I don't want him obsessing over where the hell I am."

I popped my head into three-fourteen. Kenny was seated in an orange plastic visitor's chair that looked like it was from the 1960s. There was another chair, upholstered in green faux leather with a cushion, and Barbie was seated in that. She had the cushion sitting on her lap and her arms wrapped around a large pink purse. It looked like she had normal clothes on. I mean, just jeans and a light blue t-shirt like something normal folks might wear, nothing that shouted Barbie.

"Kenny," I called, and he looked over his shoulder and then quickly stood up.

"Hey, Dev, how's it going? You got out of there okay last night?"

"Yeah, some questions and shit, it was pretty late when I got home, but I was able to grab some sleep."

"Morton okay?"

"That guy? He's doing fine. Right now, he's either chasing a tennis ball or he's taking a nap. More importantly, how are you?"

His upper lip looked about four times larger than normal, and there was some swelling on the left side of his face, but he seemed okay and, more importantly, he was smiling.

"I'm pretty good. The police were here this morning asking all sorts of questions. They showed me some pictures of those guys, but I really couldn't recognize them 'cause they were always wearing those masks, least when I saw 'em."

"They'll probably want to talk to you again, Kenny, maybe a couple more times. Not that you did anything wrong, but as they get more information from everyone, they'll just naturally have some more questions. You just tell them everything you know, and that will be a big help to them."

"Yeah, I told them about Fatty. But it didn't seem to make any sense to them."

"Fatty?"

"Yeah, right before they left me in that van. They just turned the van off, and one of them said, 'Was that Fatty's car back there on the street?' And another one said, 'I sure as hell hope not.' Then they got out of the van, took their duffel bags, and just left me there in the back until you and Morton came and found me."

"They said Fatty? You're sure about that?"

"Well, yeah, I was right there. Even though they had that hood over my head and I couldn't see, I could hear just fine." He was beginning to sound a little defensive. "They said Fatty, Dev, honest, they, they really did."

"Umm-mmm, hi, Dev," Barbie shrugged and gave me a little wave.

"How are you doing, Barbie? You okay?"

"Yeah, a little worse for the wear, but I'll make it, thanks to Ken."

"I talked to Mr. Diamond. He's going to get us a different suite. It would just be too stressful to go back into the Barbie suite right now."

Barbie smiled and nodded in agreement, then said, "Ken's been absolutely wonderful through this whole ordeal. He's even arranged for me to have an interview."

"An interview, you mean like on tv?" I looked at Ken.

"No, they're interested in hiring Barbie. Mr. Diamond said the crowds were so big when she made her appearance that they're thinking of doing something every night. Maybe even her own show."

"It would be synced with the fountain shows in the evenings," Barbie added.

"Is this for, what, a couple more days? A week?"

"No, silly, full time, permanent," she said and smiled. "Mr. Diamond has put it all together."

"They were thinking she might do a show," Kenny said, and I immediately thought the term 'show' could cover a lot of ground in Vegas. "Did you see Goose yet?"

"Yeah, as a matter of fact, I did. That's why I popped in. Well, to see you, of course, and make sure you were all right, and then to let you know I'm going to take him home. Now, do you have a way to get home, Kenny?"

"Yeah, Mr. Diamond is sending a limo for us. It should be here any minute."

"And you'll be going back to The Palms?"

"To a different suite. I can't wait to get out of these dreadful clothes," Barbie said.

"Great to see you, Kenny, really glad you're okay. You did well, everyone got out in one piece, and it's all because you used your head. You're a hero, Kenny, and we're all proud of you."

Kenny beamed.

"Barbie, what can I say? I wish you all success in your new venture. Don't forget, you've got all those winnings still tucked away over at the Bellagio."

"I've got my receipt right here," she said and patted her purse. "Thinking about a car, a pink convertible would be really fun out here."

What could I say?

"See you, Dev," Kenny said, then turned to Barbie, "Think we should check and see if the limo is out there?"

"Let's just wait for them to come up here for us. We don't want to look too anxious," Barbie said.

The nurse and Goose were waiting in the hall outside his room. "Everything go okay?"

"Yeah, yeah, Kenny's doing fine, and he's just waiting for his limo ride back to The Palms."

"And?"

"And he's going back to The Palms. Apparently, Diamond wants to talk contract with Barbie. Thinks there might be some greater marketing opportunity or something."

"You okay with that?"

"I got nothing to say about it. And believe me, it's so not a problem. Don't worry, it's completely off my radar."

Forty-seven

The flight attendant flashed a smile and asked. "Something to drink?"

I felt like asking for a couple of Jameson's but said instead, "Just a water, please."

She handed me a bottle of water, smiled, and moved on, just like all the women seem to do in my life. I went back to looking out the window from thirty thousand feet and obsessing about Barbie.

* * *

We'd been home for a little over a week, Morton and I. He was sitting in his basket in front of the file cabinet, chewing on what was left of a bright pink high heel. One of two he'd found under my bed and a pair of shoes I certainly had no use for.

I was involved in assessing the dancing ability of one of the girls in the third-floor apartment across the street. Coincidentally, she was wearing a pink thong and, I think, a smile, when she wasn't drinking from her wine glass. I was more than a little surprised, neither she nor her roommate were usually home in the middle of a weekday afternoon, and I considered myself lucky.

I adjusted the focus ever so slightly on my binoculars as she spun and dipped to music I couldn't hear, not that I was interested in the music.

"Enjoying the show?" A voice rasped from behind me.

I spun round in my office chair just in time to see Tubby Gustafson waddle into the room. Fat Freddy Zimmerman, his aide de camp, closed my office door behind him, and then the two of them oozed into the client chairs opposite my desk. Freddy took the chair with the grey duct tape.

"So how was your trip, Haskell? I trust you enjoyed yourself?"

"So far as it went, yeah, I guess it was okay. I don't think I'm exactly cut out for Vegas."

"You didn't enjoy the gambling? The crowds? The Barbie suite?"

"Well, I don't really gamble. I got tired of looking at the crowds, and I only caught a couple of fleeting glimpses of the Barbie suite," I said, wondering how much he knew.

"Pity, there's a lot going on in that town."

"Yes, sir, and most of it doesn't interest me. I think in my case, it's maybe a forty-eight-hour town, and, well, I was out there for close to a week."

"You extended your trip?"

"A bit of a complication, I was just out there a couple of days longer than planned."

"And your friend, Arthur Gander, he's doing all right?"

I wondered how he knew about Goose. "Yeah, yeah, fine. It was good to see him and be able to spend some time together."

"And doesn't he have a brother out there?"

"Yes, a younger brother, nice kid."

"I'm sure their mother over on Ashland Avenue never stops worrying about them, you know how mothers can be."

Message delivered. "They're both doing well, and I'm very sure she has nothing to worry about."

"Let's hope so," Tubby said, then groaned out of the chair and headed for the door.

"Hey, next time you're in Vegas, you should check this show out. It's supposed to be pretty good," Fat Freddy said, then tossed a full-color picture the size of a business card across my desk.

I recognized the woman lying naked on a tiger skin rug. The copy read 'Barbie, like you've never seen her before!' I just stared at the card for a very long moment, then looked at Freddy, shocked. For the first time, I noticed the gold ring on the little finger of his right hand, sporting a fairly large diamond.

"Like I said, I heard it's a pretty good show," he said and followed Tubby out the door. I watched as they walked out of the building a minute later, waited for a car to pass, then headed across the street to a black Cadillac Escalade. Fat Freddy held the door open for Tubby. Tubby must have made a comment because Freddy nodded and looked like he was laughing. As he opened the driver's door and climbed in, I recalled what Kenny said he had heard the night of the robbery; 'Was that Fatty's car back there on the street?'

Freddy waited a moment for a bus to pass, then pulled away from the curb. I raised my binoculars and focused on the bumper sticker on the rear of his Escalade. White with black copy, except the last word, that was bright red. 'I'm what happens in Vegas!'

The End

Thanks for taking the time to read
What Happens in Vegas...
Check out the sample of **Art Hound**, the next work of genius in the Dev Haskell series.

Sneak Peek

Art Hound

Second Edition

MIKE FARICY

Prologue

I cranked my neck back and forth, and it gave off an audible pop. Then I stretched my arms and legs as best I could in the front passenger seat and pulled my phone out to check the time. Just a little after six in the morning. My car was in the parking lot of the Tryst Hotel and Restaurant two rows behind Farrell Finley's red F150 pickup. Other than stepping out to relieve myself, I'd been sitting in my car since a little after nine last night in the hopes of getting a couple of shots of Farrell and the "girlfriend" he was with.

"Girlfriend" might be too strong a term. She went by the misnomer of Chastity on her escort website, and he'd paid for the privilege of her company two or three times before, at least, that was how many times I was aware of. Foolishly, he'd made those arrangements on a home computer.

I guess he didn't lie about being out of town for the night. The Tryst Hotel was a good six miles over the state line and into Wisconsin, making it about twenty-four miles from his front door in Saint Paul. I knew Farrell had to be at his desk at nine, and he had to drop Chastity off someplace back in town, so I figured I'd be able to get my pictures in the next hour or so.

The parking lot was slowly filling up with the early morning breakfast crowd. It looked like mostly regulars since it was off the interstate by a good mile, and the average age of the folks pulling in appeared to be north of sixty. At five minutes after seven, Farrell and Chastity walked out of the hotel.

Bleach-blonde Chastity looked the part in a skimpy top, exposing a midriff and love handles. She wore blue-jean cutoffs that looked like they were spray-painted on and didn't quite cover. She carried her luggage, what appeared to be a small black velvet bag probably filled with battery-operated appliances, slung over her shoulder. They were holding hands and laughing as they headed toward Farrell's pickup truck.

He was a relatively large guy with close-cropped reddish-blonde hair. He was light-skinned, as opposed to pale, with freckles, lots of freckles. I guessed he'd let himself go over the last ten plus years, and the once narrow waist now hung over his belt. That said, he was still the kind of guy you wouldn't want to push, and I certainly didn't want to this morning.

I started taking pictures using a digital camera. The time and date would appear in the lower right-hand corner of each image. They suddenly took a different route than I had expected, veering over a couple of parking places so Farrell could appraise a classic Trans Am parked in the lot. The problem with their new route was the sign touting the Tryst Hotel wouldn't show up in my pictures.

I made a command decision and quietly slipped out of my car. I slinked over about a half-dozen parking spaces to the right until I had them aligned with the hotel sign.

Click. Click. Click.

"Good God, I think this here is a sixty-nine, part of Pontiac's limited edition release. What a beauty. But I don't know if I'd be letting it sit out here in a parking lot overnight."

Click. Click. Click.

"Some idiot's liable to scratch it or open a door and hit the damn paint job."

"Hey, you know that jerky guy over there?" Chastity asked.

Click. Click

"What?"

"That weirdo over there, see him kinda hiding behind the green car. He's been taking pictures of us. Hey, creep, how 'bout this?" Chastity said, then lifted her skimpy top, exposing herself, struck a pose, and gave me the finger.

Click.

"Just what in the hell do you think you're doing, Jackass?"

Click.

Oh, oh.

Farrell started heading toward me. He wasn't huge, but he was bigger than me, and right now he didn't look happy. I started to casually walk toward my car, a 2007 Dodge Caliber. After about four paces, I figured it might make sense to just get in the car and flee the scene so I started running, as fast as I could. So did Farrell. Unfortunately, Farrell had been a high school football star, and I hadn't.

"Get him, Farrell, get him, woo-hoo, go, baby, go," Chastity screamed as she jumped up and down.

We met at the driver's door of my car.

"Who the hell are you?" Farrell shouted then punched me in the face.

"Back off, Farrell, I'm just doing my job." My head suddenly bounced off the side of the car, and I saw stars for a moment. I took a couple of quick steps back. Farrell clenched both fists, got an even meaner look on his face, and took a step toward me. I flung the car door open and caught him right between the eyes. He landed on the ground in a sitting position, looking stunned. I reached into the car, pulled the pistol out from underneath the driver's seat then calmly closed the car door.

"Hey, Farrell. No offense, but you're a real asshole. You got a wife and three kids at home, and your wife is wise to you. If I were you, I'd get my ass back to town and try and figure out how you're going to fix things if it isn't too late already."

"You can't tell me what to do."

"Hey, you listening? I just did. Now get the hell out of here before I change my mind."

He slowly got to his feet and shook his head as if to clear it. His lips were split, already swelling, he had a trail of blood dripping out of his right nostril and a large angular bruise in the middle of his forehead. "You better watch out, 'cause I'm gonna find out who the hell you are."

"You got bigger problems than me right now, Farrell. Just get in your truck and go home."

He seemed to think about that for a moment, looked at the pistol I was holding, then backed up a few paces before he turned and quickly headed for his truck. He climbed in, slammed the door, then fired up his F-150 and screeched out of the parking lot, leaving a cloud of exhaust and bleach-blonde Chastity in the dust.

"Farrell, hey Farrell, baby, wait. Wait for me, baby, wait," Chastity called. She ran after him for a car length or two, then stopped and screamed, "You worthless bastard, I'm glad you didn't get any."

Farrell's pickup raced down the road and faded into the distance.

I slipped behind the wheel of my car and headed in the same direction Farrell had just gone, but nowhere near as fast. I watched Chastity in the rearview mirror as she headed back into the Tryst Hotel.

One

Later that day, just across town . . .

"Are you f'ing kidding me? You painted that on my dining room wall?" Colleen asked.

Demarcus Cantrell stood back and admired his work, a naked woman eating an apple lying on what appeared to be a massive dinner platter. He'd even incorporated her mother's china pattern into the platter. He decided some attention was still required, the shadowed area beneath the right breast, and perhaps just the slightest bit of warmth added to the lips, but otherwise, yet another work of artistic genius.

"The room just needed something. I can't always be restricted to a small canvas, my precious. Just think of the value it will add to the house."

"Value added to the house? My house? That's it, Demarcus, I've had it. I want you out of here, right now."

"Precious, relax, calm down. We've both had a long workday. Now what do you say you make me some fresh coffee and both of us lunch while I clean up?"

"Did you hear me? I said, get the hell out of my house. Now," she screamed, then grabbed an easel and a canvas from the corner and marched toward the door.

"Precious, now calm down."

"My name is Colleen. You call me 'Precious' again, and I'm going to stab you. I'm coming off a double shift, and you've spent the last sixteen hours painting a naked woman on my dining room wall." She tore the front door open and tossed the easel into the yard, then flipped the canvas out on top of it. "Get moving, mister. I have had it. I've paid the freight around here for over four months, and this is what I come home to? You are so done."

"I think we should talk. You don't seem to understand."

She ran into the kitchen, and a moment later, he heard a drawer being pulled open. She was back in the dining room, eyes flaring and baring her teeth. She held a very large, very sharp butcher knife.

"Whoa now, Precious, err, umm, Colleen, calm down. Maybe you'd like it better if she was blonde. I can change that."

"Ahhh," she screamed, red-faced as she slashed at him with the knife.

"Calm down, my, I mean, Colleen. Just calm down."

"Killing you would be so simple right now and probably the only way to bring any value to your wretched, worthless paintings. Now, I'm going upstairs to the guest room for some much-needed sleep. I'm taking this knife with me. When I wake up, if you and all your paintings are still here, I'm really going to kill you."

"Darling, I think you may be overreacting."

"Please don't think. It drives me crazy when you try and think. Please. Do. Not. Think," she screamed.

"Okay, okay," he said, pulling a chair between them for added protection.

"I'm going to close my eyes. I've worked a double shift, and right now, I have a very, very short fuse. For your own good, do not be here when I wake up. Goodbye, Demarcus. It's been a real education," she said, then turned and headed up to the bedroom.

He examined his work for a moment, decided it would only take a moment or two to warm the smile and attend to the shadow before he packed his belongings, and so set to work. An hour later, he stepped back from the wall and viewed his creation with an air of satisfaction. Yeah, he was definitely on to something here. He decided to take a couple of photos and upload them into a file. If Colleen didn't wish to participate, well, that would be her loss. He thought for a moment and wondered where he could go.

Two

Heidi raised her eyebrows and gave me a look. "Oh, come on, Dev, a poetry reading, it'll be fun. God only knows you could use the culture, plus there just might be something in it for you afterward." I immediately got on board.

Finally, it was Friday night after what had been a couple of grueling weeks for both of us. Heidi was dealing with some initial public offering she'd promoted to investors that was finally beginning to perform after two weeks of heated phone calls from people with too much money and way too much time.

Me? Let's see. I got dumped by a woman named Margo before the relationship even got off the ground. I thought things were starting to look up when she left me the polite phone message at four in the morning that said, 'Things aren't working out,' followed by another message two minutes later where she just screamed, 'Fuck you,' and hung up.

I drove over to her house that night with Morton, my golden retriever, serving as a witness, hoping to calm Margo down. That thought quickly went from bad to really bad when she began screaming and frightened Morton, who ended up leaving a puddle on her kitchen floor. The two of us were out the door about ninety seconds after that. My only thought was if I heard the screen door open behind me as I walked to my car it was everyone for themselves because I was going to run.

Anyway, that was the highlight of my social life. Business-wise, the good news was I got the somewhat compromising photos of Farrell engaged in a stupid extramarital affair. The bad news was he was a one-time high school football star and caught up with me.

"How does that eye feel?" Heidi asked. "It still looks pretty sore."

"The swelling has gone down. I can touch it now, and it doesn't hurt, too much. The blurry vision has pretty much disappeared." I was driving us in Heidi's car to the poetry reading. Some high school friend of hers who had published her fifth or sixth book of poems. I'd never even heard of the woman, let alone the poetry books, but then again, I'm pretty much out of the demographic, well, unless the poem happens to rhyme with Nantucket.

"I think that's the place up there on the corner," Heidi said. She half pointed to a two-story stucco building on the corner. Illegible graffiti in black spray paint ran along the side of the building. One of the front windows was covered with a sheet of plywood hosting more spray-painted graffiti, this time in red.

"That dive on the corner?"

"Yeah, I guess. I mean, it looks kind of dumpy," Heidi said.

"Then it fits right into the neighborhood, that church we just passed a block back had a 'No Loitering' sign out in front." I pulled alongside the curb and parked behind a shiny black Mercedes, probably the neighborhood pimp's car.

"We better hurry, I don't want to miss anything," Heidi said and jumped out of the car. I checked the backseat to make sure nothing was left in the car because it wouldn't be there when we returned, and we'd no doubt have a window to replace. "Are you coming?" she called from the sidewalk.

We hurried inside, not that we needed to. With our attendance, the crowd, including poet, author, and reader, Eunice, increased to nine people. Her first poem, I can't recall the title, went on for twenty-three minutes, and didn't rhyme. When she was finished, everyone gave polite applause except for me, only because I'd drifted off to sleep. Heidi elbowed me as she clapped. "That was wonderful," she said and glared at me.

I got the message and fought to remain awake for the next hour and a half through a few more monotone readings. Finally, Eunice slid off her stool and took a deep bow. I clapped, but only because she was finally finished. Heidi purchased her book and had Eunice sign it. Then we stepped over to the hors d'oeuvres table, actually a card table with an open bottle of Jameson and a stack of plastic cups. I poured myself an hors d'oeuvre.

"You're the only one drinking," Heidi said under her breath as she smiled at a well-dressed older couple walking past. The guy made his way to the card table and poured himself a glass.

"I'm the only one who's recovered. Everyone else is still numb from the neck up."

"Mrs. Martin," Heidi said as the older woman approached. "I'm Heidi."

"Yes, yes, of course, Heidi. It's been so long. How wonderful to see you. And thank you so much for supporting Eunice."

"My pleasure. Very interesting."

"Mmm-mmm," the woman said and then looked in my direction. "And is this, your husband?"

"A friend of mine, Dev Haskell. He's been interested in Eunice's work. Dev, this is Eunice's mom. She always took such good care of us when we were absolutely awful teenage girls."

"Oh, nothing of the sort, now stop," the woman laughed and extended her hand. "How nice to meet you, Mr. Hassle."

I shook her hand just as the guy I guessed was her husband joined us with his drink.

"Dev, this is Eunice's father," Heidi said.

He raised his glass in my direction but didn't say anything. The ladies had two minutes of worthless conversation, and then Eunice's father downed his Jameson, and they departed.

"You want to say something to Eunice?" I said and finished the last of my drink.

"No, she doesn't like to be hassled by fans."

"What? Hassled?"

"If you're finished, we should just go."

"Did I miss something?"

"Dev?"

Three

Heidi wedged two pillows behind her and sat up in bed. My Golden Retriever, Morton, had snuck up onto the bed and taken over the spot where I'd slept. I handed her a cup of coffee, and she took a sip. "Mmm-mmm, thanks. What's that I smell?"

"I'm cooking you breakfast."

"Pancakes?"

"Yeah, blueberry pancakes, with real maple syrup and some smoked bacon. You just sip your coffee and take your time. I'll call you when it's ready, maybe fifteen minutes or so."

"Oh, you're so sweet, Dev."

"Well, sorry if I didn't catch on to the cultural stuff last night. I just—"

"Oh, God, I'm sorry I dragged you to that. Wasn't it awful?"

"Awful? I thought you liked it?"

"Liked it? Are you kidding? Oh my God, it was just dreadful. They always are."

"Well then, why did we even go?"

"I always try to support Eunice. We've been friends since junior high."

"But you don't seem to have anything in common with her. You didn't even talk to her."

"I know, I know. We were really close, once, and then she took a strange turn, she started hanging with the wrong crowd, got into drugs. After high school, we went in totally opposite directions. She's recovered now, at least I think she is, but the damage is there. Oh, she used to be so talented and fun and—"

"And no offense, but she's a real downer. Those poems, they didn't even rhyme. And then she doesn't want people talking to her at the end? Really strange."

"Yeah, including her parents. She doesn't want to talk to them. It upsets her. Maybe it reminds her of what could have been if she wasn't such a mess, but that's not nice. I don't mean it like that. I know, I know. I keep going to these things hoping someday I'll walk in and there my old girlfriend will be, smiling and joking. I don't know. It's just so sad. I don't know what it would take to get her back if it can even be done."

"What do her folks think?"

"God bless them, they've had years of heartache. She was bright, intelligent, fun, interesting, and then, eventually, a burnout. Their only child and, well, you saw."

"Grim. I better get back to breakfast. Take your time. Morton, you bum, come on, you can go outside."

"Oh, he can stay."

"No way. Just close the bedroom door when you come down so he doesn't eat your thong again. Come on, Morton, let's go."

Morton took his time, hopping off the bed. He stretched on the floor for a long moment, giving me a look to see if I'd head downstairs so he could hop back up next to Heidi.

"Come on, Morton, get going," I said, and he grudgingly followed. He lingered near the front door for a long moment and gave a loud bark.

"No, come on, out the back, let's go." I had to call him once again from the kitchen before he finally followed. I figured he was angling for a walk, but he seemed to change his mind once he stepped into the kitchen and realized there was bacon on the stove.

"Outside first, then we'll see about breakfast." He hurried outside and was back at the door after just a minute or two.

I called Heidi down for breakfast. She walked into the kitchen wearing my black Ramones t-shirt. Thankfully, just short enough not to cover. "You closed the bedroom door?"

"Mmm-hmm. This looks great," she said, as I slid a plate of blueberry pancakes and smoked bacon across the counter to her, then filled up her coffee mug. "Bon Appétit."

"Oh, God, French. Who knew?"

"It's all that culture I absorbed last night."

"Yeah, right."

We talked for a long time over breakfast. She grabbed a shower while I cleaned up in the kitchen, then came down all dressed just as I finished up.

"You want another coffee? Don't feel like you have to go."

"I've got a couple hours of office work I have to get done."

"It's Saturday, take a break."

"Wish I could, but I need to get this wrapped up before Monday. I've investors coming in at nine."

"You sure?"

"Yeah, but I'll take a rain check."

"You got it," I said. "Come on. I'll walk you to the door."

"Oh, ever the gentleman," she laughed. She gave me a quick kiss at the door, then patted Morton on the head as I opened the door.

"Ufff, ouch, God," the man grunted as he fell into the front entry, and his head bounced off the floor.

Heidi shrieked.

Morton barked and ran behind Heidi.

I just shouted, "Demarcus? What the hell are you doing here?"

Four

We'd been hauling easels, tubes of oil paints, canvases…a lot of canvas, a toaster, a half-dozen ceramic angelfish to hang on the wall, a stained glass lamp with a brass naked lady base and just an awful lot of junk into the living room for the past half-hour while Demarcus told me the story, at least his version of the story. Just now, I was carrying four more canvas paintings and leaning them against the dozen or so of the same size I'd already stacked against the wall.

Demarcus had hold of a faux-leather, high-backed office chair patched in three different places with fluorescent green duct tape. He rolled it in the door behind me then pushed it across the entry with his foot, where it bounced against the wall.

"I don't know, man, it's like I said, she just all of a sudden went off the deep end and was threatening to kill me. The next thing I know, she's heading up to the guest room with a butcher knife, telling me I have to be gone when she wakes up. Based on the circumstances, I decided it maybe wasn't the best time to try and reason with her."

"Maybe she was just, you know, exhausted from do-ing that double shift."

"Yeah, maybe, but I've been sensing something like this for quite some time. She's mentioned me getting a job, seems like every other day for the past month. Christ, can't she tell I'm an artist? I had canvases stored in every room on the first floor. I don't know," he said, then shook his head, suggesting none of it made any sense.

"You guys got financial trouble? I don't need to know specifics, but that can add a lot of stress to any situation."

"Well, it would certainly help if I could sell some of my artwork. But she knew that was going to be difficult when I suggested I move in with her. I mean, it seemed like a good idea at the time. After all, she's really hot. Hell, now I'm thinking she just wanted some idiot to shovel the sidewalk or cut the damn grass. You know?"

"You cut the grass and shoveled her sidewalk?"

"No. God, are you kidding? First of all, when I feel the need for artistic expression, I have to pay attention, that comes first and foremost. I'm a professional, after all. Then the other thing is, if I throw my back out using a snow shovel or pushing the damn lawnmower, that's sure not going to do much for my artistic career, now is it?"

"Yeah, but you know, maybe if you did a couple of those things around the place, it might maybe calm her down. It's hard keeping a house up. She's working, pulling double shifts, there's always going to be something that needs to be fixed or replaced in any house."

"Come on, and she's always worried about keeping her figure. She goes to the 'Y' almost every day. I thought I was helping out by having her do some physical labor around the place. It's free. She doesn't even have to pay a membership fee or anything. But, oh no, that won't do. She'd much rather read me the riot act, ruin the mood. I don't know, I can't figure her out."

I more or less missed that last part since I was outside bringing in two suitcases and a very heavy duffel bag. One of the suitcases was dark blue with creamy-colored or maybe just yellowed leather along the sides and looked to be about sixty years old. The other was black and looked somewhat better, although it was missing a set of wheels, which meant I had to pick it up instead of rolling the thing. The large duffel bag, absolutely crammed with clothes, was strapped over my shoulder. The strap felt like it was cutting into the side of my neck.

"Oh, yeah, you could probably drag that duffel bag back by your washing machine. I need to do some of that laundry. Feel free to throw a load in while you're back there."

"No, thanks. Hey, thought you were painting bowls of fruit, when did you start doing that stuff?" I nodded toward the stack of canvases leaning against the wall. All of them looked like they'd been used as a drop cloth. Just splatters of different colored paint, it looked like maybe three colors to a canvas, red, white and black, or orange, yellow and green. Two of them had maybe five colors splattered across them. Rolls of canvas, apparently all yellowed with age or else they'd been out in the sun too long, were now standing in two corners of my living room.

"Well, I did these for a year or two. I guess maybe a little too advanced for this town."

"A year or two? How many did you do?"

"How many? Those twelve there, I was on a roll, cranking out one a month, really pushing it."

"One a month?"

"Yeah, like I said, I've been really pushing it."

"You sold any?"

"That's not the real point. And, before you say anything, Colleen bitched about that, too, so whatever it is, I've already heard what you were about to say. Dev, I don't expect you to get this, but I'm constantly pushing the frontiers, and first of all, you have to be in the mood, really in the mood, to create these. Here, check this one out," he said, picking up a canvas from the stack. It was a black background, with drips and splashes of red, white, and purple. "What does it say to you?"

I wanted to say something along the lines of 'bullshit.' I figured I could do one of those things in about five minutes with my eyes closed. "Man's inhumanity to man?"

"Good, very good. Wow, I'm surprised. Actually, it represents the juxtaposition of mother earth to life, at least as we know it. Get it? Dark space and the very beginnings of life forms from which we've all descended. You go back far enough, we're all related."

I shook my head and wondered who in the hell would buy something like that, let alone hang it up somewhere. "You sell any of those?"

"I just got done saying, it's not about selling them. My talent has nothing to do with the monetary factor."

"So, then, why were you doing it?" Right now, I was thinking if I had been Colleen, I would have done this a long time ago. No, check that, I would never have gotten involved with Demarcus.

"Why was I doing it? Dev, it has to be done."

"But, then, when did you start doing the nude thing, like on Colleen's dining room wall?"

"That's been a recent occurrence. If you're interested, I'll email you an image."

"Yeah, I'd like to see it."

"Anyway, that's not important. This is the future," he said, then carefully set the splattered canvas back in the stack.

I looked around the place. My living room was crammed full of junk, all of which belonged to Demarcus. "So, ahh, how long are you planning to stay?"

"Shouldn't be more than a day or two, just until I get a couple of different options worked out. Say, you want to grab those suitcases and take them up to your guest room? I'm gonna grab a beer and make a sandwich. You want anything?"

To be continued...

Thanks for taking the time to check out the sample of **Art Hound**. Sounds like Dev has his hand full, but then no good deed goes unpunished. Better click on the link below and grab your copy to see how things end up....

Books by Mike Faricy
Crime Fiction Firsts

A boxset of the first four books in four crime fiction series:

Russian Roulette; Dev Haskell series
Welcome; Jack Dillon Dublin Tales series
Corridor Man; Corridor Man series
Reduced Ransom! Hot Shot series

The following titles comprise the Dev Haskell series:

Russian Roulette: Case 1
Mr. Swirlee: Case 2
Bite Me: Case 3
Bombshell: Case 4
Tutti Frutti: Case 5
Last Shot: Case 6
Ting-A-Ling: Case 7
Crickett: Case 8
Bulldog: Case 9
Double Trouble: Case 10
Yellow Ribbon: Case 11
Dog Gone: Case 12
Scam Man: Case 13
Foiled: Case 14
What Happens in Vegas… Case 15
Art Hound: Case 16
The Office: Case 17

Star Struck: Case 18
International Incident: Case 19
Guest From Hell: Case 20
Art Attack: Case 21
Mystery Man: Case 22
Bow-Wow Rescue: Case 23
Cold Case: Case 24
Cash Up Front: Case 25
Dream House: Case 26
Alley Katz: Case 27
The Big Gamble: Case 28
Bad to the Bone: Case 29
Silencio!: Case 30
Surprise, Surprise: Case 31
Hit & Run: Case 32
Suspect Santa: Case 33
P.I. Apprentice: Case 34
Rebel Without a Clue: Case 35

The following titles are Dev Haskell novellas:
Dollhouse
The Dance
Pixie
Fore!
Twinkle Toes
(*a Dev Haskell short story*)

The following are Dev Haskell Boxsets:
Dev Haskell Boxset 1-3
Dev Haskell Boxset 4-6
Dev Haskell Boxset 7-9
Dev Haskell Boxset 10-12
Dev Haskell Boxset 13-15
Dev Haskell Boxset 16-18
Dev Haskell Boxset 19-21
Dev Haskell Boxset 22-24
Dev Haskell Boxset 25-27
Dev Haskell Boxset 28-30
Dev Haskell Boxset 1-7
Dev Haskell Boxset 8-14
Dev Haskell Boxset 15-19
Dev Haskell Boxset 20-24
Dev Haskell Boxset 25-29

The following titles comprise the Jack Dillon Dublin Tales series:
Welcome
Jack Dillon Dublin Tale 1
Sweet Dreams
Jack Dillon Dublin Tale 2
Mirror Mirror
Jack Dillon Dublin Tale 3
Silver Bullet
Jack Dillon Dublin Tale 4
Fair City Blues
Jack Dillon Dublin Tale 5

Spade Work
Jack Dillon Dublin Tale 6
Madeline Missing
Jack Dillon Dublin Tale 7
Mistaken Identity
Jack Dillon Dublin Tale 8
Picture Perfect
Jack Dillon Dublin Tale 9
Dublin Moon
Jack Dillon Dublin Tale 10
Mystery Woman
Jack Dillon Dublin Tale 11
Second Chance
Jack Dillon Dublin Tale 12
Payback Brother
Jack Dillon Dublin Tale 13
The Heist
Jack Dillon Dublin Tale 14
Jewels To Kill For
Jack Dillon Dublin Tale 15
Retirement Scheme
Jack Dillon Dublin Tale 16
The Collector
Jack Dillon Dublin Tale 17

Jack Dillon Dublin Tales Boxsets:
Jack Dillon Dublin Tales 1-3
Jack Dillon Dublin Tales 4-6
Jack Dillon Dublin Tales 1-5

Jack Dillon Dublin Tales 1-7
Jack Dillon Dublin Tales 6-10

The following titles comprise the Hotshot series;
Reduced Ransom! Second Edition
Finders Keepers! Second Edition
Bankers Hours Second Edition
Chow Down Second Edition
Moonlight Dance Academy Second Edition
Irish Dukes (Fight Card Series)
written under the pseudonym Jack Tunney

The following titles comprise the Corridor Man series:
Corridor Man
Corridor Man 2: Opportunity knocks
Corridor Man 3: The Dungeon
Corridor Man 4: Dead End
Corridor Man 5: Finger
Corridor Man 6: Exit Strategy
Corridor Man 7: Trunk Music
Corridor Man 8: Birthday Boy
Corridor Man 9: Boss Man
Corridor Man 10: Bye Bye Bobby

Corridor Man novellas:
Corridor Man: Valentine
Corridor Man: Auditor
Corridor Man: Howling

Corridor Man: Spa Day

The following are Corridor Man Boxsets:
Corridor Man Boxset 1-3
Corridor Man Boxset 1-5
Corridor Man Boxset 6-9

All books are available on Amazon.com
Thank you!

Contact the author:
- Email: mikefaricyauthor@gmail.com
- Twitter: @Mikefaricybooks
- Facebook: Mike Faricy Author
- Website: http://www.mikefaricybooks.com

Published by

MJF Publishing